Writer Guild of America East
Certified Registration Number: I371390
Registration Date: 06/15/2024

ISBN: 9798328910675

Cover: "Migration", Oil painting by Tito Lugo
Printed in the United States of America

...to my wife Wanda, from the moment I looked into your eyes, I felt in my soul the premonition of this immense love that now surrounds us, like a river flowing eternally, destined to unite our lives in an endless dance...

Precognition
Tito Lugo MD©

I

Lucas Presagios possessed a singular gift, although he was not yet aware of its true extent. His existence had been marked by a constant restlessness; a burden that seemed unsustainable. From a young age, Lucas had been haunted by fleeting visions, glimpses of events that would occur in the near future. These premonitions appeared sporadically and intermittently, like shadows dancing at the edge of his consciousness, always present when he least expected them.

On one occasion, Lucas vividly recalled one of his earliest and most disturbing visions. He was a teenager when he fell into a brief but intense trance, during which he saw a six-year-old girl being kidnapped from a humble home. The scene unfolded with terrifying clarity: unknown men were forcing the girl into a luxurious Mercedes car. However, as the vision progressed toward its brutal conclusion, Lucas could not discern the faces of the perpetrators. The girl was the daughter of a district judge who had sentenced a confessed murderer to 150 years in prison.

The place where the girl was held captive was shrouded in shadows and confusing details. Although the outlines of the room were blurry in his mind, there was something ominously familiar about the site. Years later, in a desperate attempt to free himself from the torment of his precognition, Lucas visited that very room. As he crossed the threshold, a shiver ran down his spine. It was as if he had been there before, experiencing a déjà vu so intense that it left him breathless.

The cruel murder of the girl sparked an uproar in the communities that knew the family. The news spread quickly, and the collective shock was palpable. Lucas, trapped in the impotence of his visions, felt consumed by guilt and despair. Knowing what was going to happen and being unable to intervene was a burden that tormented him day and night.

The vision had left him scarred for life. He painfully remembered the expression of terror on the girl's face, her voice silenced by fear, and the relentless coldness of the men who took her from her home. Every detail of that vision replayed in his mind like an incessant echo, reminding him of the cruel reality of his gift. Not only was he able to foresee the future, but he could also experience the suffering of others without being able to do anything to prevent it.

From that young age, Lucas knew his life would never be normal. The visions not only showed him possible futures but also plunged him into the depths of pain and despair of those he saw. Each new vision was an open wound, a reminder of his inability to change the destiny unfolding before his eyes.

As he grew older, he tried various ways to rid himself of his ability, seeking answers in ancient books, consulting scholars, and exploring esoteric methods. But precognition remained an inseparable part of his being, a gift and a curse that pursued him relentlessly. His journey to understand and, perhaps one day, control his ability was just beginning. In his heart, Lucas harbored the hope that one day he could use his gift for good, to prevent tragedies and save lives, instead of being a mere helpless spectator of the horrors to come.

Sometimes, these visions brought with them a strange comfort, a sense of relief that enveloped him like a warm embrace in the midst of chaos. Other times, however, they plunged him into an abyss of unease, revealing tragedies and evils that left him paralyzed with terror. The truth was that these premonitions, whether good or bad, tormented Lucas incessantly, a constant reminder that there was something in his life he did not fully understand.

Each vision was an enigma, a piece of a puzzle that Lucas did not yet know how to solve. Sometimes, he saw accidents just before they happened, being able to warn people around him and prevent disaster. Other times, he witnessed moments of happiness and success, scenes that materialized with chilling precision. But there were also dark nights when he glimpsed acts of cruelty and violence, leaving an indelible mark of despair in his mind.

Lucas had tried to ignore these visions, attributing them to mere coincidences or the whims of his imagination. However, as he grew older, the premonitions became more vivid and harder to dismiss. Over time, he began to wonder if there was a purpose behind this strange phenomenon. Why him? What meaning did these visions have for his life and the lives of those around him?

One day, after a particularly intense series of visions, Lucas decided he could no longer live in uncertainty. He had to find answers, understand the origin of his gift, and discover how to control it. Thus, he embarked on a journey of self-discovery, an odyssey full of mystery and danger, where each step brought him closer to the truth and, at the same time, plunged him into a world of intrigues and ancient secrets.

In his quest, Lucas would encounter enigmatic characters, guardians of ancient traditions and forgotten wisdoms. He would face challenges that would test not only his ability to foresee the future but also his courage and determination. Little by little, Lucas would begin to unravel the true power of his gift and the crucial role he was destined to play in a conflict much greater than he had ever imagined.

Thus began the adventure of Lucas Presagios, a journey that would define not only his destiny but also that of all those whose lives were intertwined with the mysterious thread of his visions.

Lucas' surname, "Presagios," had its roots in the ancient region of Toledo, Spain, a place shrouded in legends and mysteries. For generations, his family had been known for their ability to foresee future events, a gift that placed them in a unique and often unsettling position within society. According to stories passed down by word of mouth, the founder of the family, Santiago Presagios, was a renowned seer in the court of King Charles II during the 17th century. His ability to foresee natural disasters and political conflicts made him both a respected and feared figure.

Charles II, nicknamed "The Bewitched," was the last monarch of the Habsburg dynasty in Spain. His reign was marked by numerous health problems as well as political and economic crises. He frequently consulted Don Santiago Presagios about the future of these crises, and thanks to his skill with words, Don Santiago managed to soothe the king's concerns about the future of his reign.

Santiago Presagios was not only an indispensable advisor to the monarch but also a man shrouded in an aura of mysticism. His visions were so precise that some considered him an intermediary between the world of mortals and the unknown. It was said that Santiago could see devastating storms weeks before they formed and anticipate military movements with such accuracy that he saved the kingdom from countless conflicts. However, this gift did not come without a price. The ability to foresee the future was a heavy burden, often plunging him into deep states of melancholy and exhaustion.

Despite Don Santiago Presagios' efforts, Charles II could not escape his fate. His health, always fragile, rapidly deteriorated, and not even his advisor's reassuring words could change the course of events. Spain's political and economic situation continued to worsen, with the kingdom losing influence and facing internal rebellions. In his final years, Charles II suffered from constant illnesses and extreme weakness, preventing him from effectively governing. In 1700, without leaving an heir, his death marked the end of the Habsburg dynasty in Spain and triggered the War of Spanish Succession, a conflict that would reshape the political map of Europe.

Over the centuries, the Presagios family maintained this ability intermittently, passing the gift from generation to generation sporadically. Some family members never experienced a vision in their lives, while others were haunted by them from a young age. The stories of their ancestors were filled with episodes where their premonitions had saved lives or prevented catastrophes, but also with moments where their visions had driven them to the brink of madness.

Thus, the gift finally came to Lucas Presagios, our dear and suffering protagonist. Lucas grew up listening to the stories of his lineage, tales of great deeds and terrible sufferings, but he always thought they were just that: stories. However, as his own visions began to manifest, the reality of his legacy became inescapable. Lucas' premonitions were a constant reminder of the heavy heritage he carried, a responsibility he had not asked for but could not ignore.

Caught between everyday life and glimpses of an uncertain future, Lucas struggled to find balance. The visions were a constant torment, disturbing his peace and leaving him with a sense of helplessness. He didn't know how to control them or use them for a greater good, and each day without answers increased his despair.

The Presagios legacy was not just a gift but a curse that isolated him from the rest of the world. However, deep down, Lucas felt there was a greater purpose for his ability, something he did not yet fully understand but was determined to discover. Thus, with the history of his family resonating in his mind, Lucas embarked on a journey to unravel the mystery of his destiny, a path full of adventures, dangers, and revelations that would lead him to confront not only his lineage's past but also the future of all humanity.

Lucas had to return to his hometown, Toledo. There, he needed to speak with his relatives residing in Spain. His ancestors and the surrounding stories were his compass, guiding his steps toward a destiny he did not yet fully understand. This journey was his plan, though fate sometimes plays tricks that are hard to comprehend.

Recently, Lucas had divorced his wife, Claribel Previs. Claribel was a dark-skinned Creole, known for her vibrant energy and thunderous personality. Her presence did not go unnoticed: an exotic beauty with a majestic body that captured the gazes of men and women alike. Her exuberance and vitality were so irresistible that they left a lasting impression on those who knew her.

Claribel was the ideal of the plastic surgeons of the time. With a monumental bust, a wasp waist, and a round, voluminous rear, her figure embodied the beauty standards of the moment. Her Afro-Antillean ancestry gave her a brown complexion and jet-black hair with unruly curls. Her eyes, a penetrating young olive color, completed an appearance that captured the attention and admiration of everyone around her.

After a somewhat tumultuous romantic relationship of almost two years, Claribel and Lucas decided to unite their lives in marriage. They promised to care for each other in good times and bad and never to separate what God had joined. However, those promises, often wrapped in the rhetoric of eternal love, turned out to be illusory. The same words that were meant to seal their union became chains that made their divorce just another statistic in a world where separations are four times more common than marriages.

The marriage to Claribel had been an emotional roller coaster, full of passionate highs and devastating lows. Lucas remembered the moments when their love seemed invincible, an unstoppable force that connected them on a deep level. But he also remembered the fights, the shouting, and the pain of two souls who, despite their love, could not find a common path. The separation was inevitable, and although it left deep scars, it also offered Lucas a new perspective on life and his purpose.

Now, with the weight of the past still present in his heart, Lucas prepared for his journey to Toledo. He hoped to find answers among his relatives and the stories of his ancestors.

Perhaps in those ancient lands, steeped in history and mysticism, he could discover more about his gift and how to control it.

The journey to Toledo was not just a physical return but also a spiritual and emotional one. Lucas needed to reconnect with his roots, understand the legacy of the Presagios family, and find his place in that long line of seers. The history of his family, full of mysteries and hidden powers, could be the key to unlocking his potential and finding the peace he so desperately sought.

Thus, with his mind full of questions and his heart laden with hope and fear, Lucas embarked on his journey. He knew the path would not be easy, but he was determined to face any challenge that came his way. This journey to Toledo would mark the beginning of a new stage in his life, a stage in which he could finally discover who he truly was and what he was destined to do with his gift.

Fate, with all its twists and turns, had plans for Lucas Presagios, and he was ready to face them, determined to unravel the secrets hidden in the heart of his lineage and in the dark corners of his own soul.

Claribel could not tolerate Lucas' psychic delusions and mental escapes. It wasn't that they openly fought, but rather that he would sink into trances while she spoke to him, and when he returned, he did so agitated and disoriented. She, completely ignored in the middle of a conversation, found herself recounting an important matter when, suddenly, Lucas would get lost in his astral world, needing help to overcome a visionary crisis. Claribel was not willing to deal with these minutiae. If at least Lucas' visions could provide some economic benefit, she might have considered staying. However, that was not the case.

Many suitors, even during her marriage, eagerly waited to immerse themselves in the ecstasy of passion with Claribel. That body needed better use. One after another, they filled her head with promises and macabre tales about the future that made her tremble with fear. The poor woman, with her majestic body and imposing presence, lived tormented by the possibility that Lucas might someday predict her fortune, perhaps recognizing in one of those dreams the winning lottery numbers. But the reality was very different. Lucas could not foresee situations governed by the law of probabilities and chance, like lottery numbers. His visions were fragmented, composed of silhouettes and shadows, almost never numbers or symbols that could translate into wealth.

Lucas' visions were a constant enigma. Although they sometimes showed glimpses of future events, they were generally confusing and difficult to interpret. His gift did not follow a clear logic, making it even more frustrating for both him and Claribel. The uncertainty about the true purpose of his visions and his inability to use them practically fueled their discontent.

The main problem was that Lucas couldn't control his premonitions, that ability that seemed more like a curse than a gift, a persistent intruder in his mind that left him breathless. "Why worry about something you think won't happen?" he wondered if it always happens, and it happens with a precision that borders on the macabre. That certainty of inevitable destiny plunged him into an unbearable state of anguish, like a heavy fog that never lifted.

Claribel, in her exuberant vitality and relentless pragmatism, did not understand Lucas, could not comprehend the internal struggle that consumed him every time his visions took hold of him. For her, everything was simple, as clear as water: if something doesn't work, you discard it, you remove it from your life like a stone in your shoe. So, she decided it was best to get out of this situation that was going nowhere, to cut her losses and leave behind the burden of Lucas' premonitions.

Lucas, for his part, was trapped in an endless cycle of visions and realities, never knowing when one would give way to the other. The premonitions came without warning, robbing him of control and plunging him into scenes he didn't want to see, into futures he would rather not know. And then there was Claribel, always there, always present, but increasingly distant, as if each of Lucas' visions was another brick in the wall that was rising between them.

Claribel had tried several times to understand and support Lucas, but her efforts always ended in despair. Each trance of Lucas made her feel more alone and helpless, increasing her resentment. She didn't see the benefit of living with a man trapped in a world of shadows and forebodings with no clear direction. The constant wait for a change that never came eroded her patience and love.

Lucas, for his part, suffered immensely seeing how his visions affected his personal life. Each trance left him exhausted and full of anguish, knowing that his inability to control his gift was destroying his marriage. He felt Claribel's gaze, laden with frustration and hopelessness, as a weight on his shoulders. The pain of not being able to offer her the stability and future she desired ate away at him inside.

Finally, the distance between them became insurmountable. Claribel decided she could no longer live in that emotional roller coaster, where each day was a struggle against the unknown. The suitors, with their promises of a simpler and more passionate life, became an irresistible temptation. Claribel opted for a safer path, leaving behind Lucas and his gift, which he had never asked for and which seemed more a curse than a gift.

In the end, Claribel found a new partner just two weeks after leaving Lucas. A man who, according to her, surpassed her former husband in every imaginable way. This new man had an imposing stature, an enviable economic position, properties everywhere, and luxury cars that gleamed under the sun. Compared to him, poor good-for-nothing Lucas was an insignificance, an annoying flea in the ear of a great dog that, with a simple movement of its paws, got rid of it effortlessly.

Claribel, with her exuberance and beauty, had quickly found someone who met her impudent, material, and social expectations. This new man enveloped her in a life of opulence and security, a life Claribel had always desired, but that Lucas could never provide. She plunged into her new existence with the same intensity with which she had abandoned the previous one, leaving behind any trace of the dark and stormy days with Lucas.

This new macho penetrated her without shame, fulfilling with a wild passion that seemed to erase any vestige of the past. For Claribel, it was all that poor mind needed: a good house, a luxury car, elegant dresses, sumptuous dinners, sparkling jewelry, and good sex. These were the pillars on which she built her happiness, the tangible elements that filled her life with satisfaction and security.

The presence of the new passionate lover transformed her existence into a whirlwind of luxury, semen, and comfort. Each day she woke up in a softer bed, in a bigger house, surrounded by the things she had always wanted. Her previous life with Lucas, with his disturbing visions and constant uncertainty, faded like a bad dream. Now, reality was bright and clear, a succession of golden days where every material need was effortlessly met.

Claribel enjoyed dinners at the most exclusive restaurants, trips to exotic destinations, and the unwavering attention of her new lover, especially in their marital bed. Her new life was far from Lucas' shadows and trances, and every new piece of jewelry in her collection was a reaffirmation that she had made the right decision. Her body, adored and desired, was now the center of a universe where every wish was fulfilled.

For Claribel, this change was not just an improvement but a liberation. She had rid herself of the nightmares of Lucas' visions, his inability to maintain a conversation without getting lost in inexplicable trances, the constant uncertainty that defined her life with him. Now, each day was a reaffirmation of her decision to leave behind what had tied her to a fate she did not want.

Lucas, for his part, was no more than a blurry memory, a shadow of the past that was quickly fading. For Claribel, he had been a transitional phase, a stage full of unfulfilled promises and broken expectations. This new man represented the opposite: stability, luxury, and a life without the interruptions of untimely premonitions. Her new relationship was an affirmation that she had made the right decision, that the world still offered her what she deserved.

Meanwhile, Lucas continued his journey to Toledo, carrying the weight of his heritage and the loneliness that now enveloped him. News of Claribel's new life reached his ears like a distant echo, a reminder of what he had lost but also of what had never truly been his. Each step he took towards his hometown was a step further from that chapter of his life, one he was determined to leave behind as he sought answers to his personal enigma.

The comparison between Lucas and Claribel's new lover was inevitable, but in his quest for peace and understanding, Lucas began to realize that their paths were different. His worth did not lie in luxury cars or properties, but in something much deeper, something he did not yet fully understand but was determined to discover. The journey to Toledo was not just a physical one but also a journey towards self-knowledge and the acceptance of his gift.

Claribel had found her path, one that veered away from the shadows and mysteries of Lucas' visions. Now, it was Lucas' turn to find his own, to discover the true purpose of his ability and finally find the peace he so desperately sought. Deep in his heart, he knew his destiny awaited him in Toledo, among the stories and secrets of his ancestors, and that there, perhaps, he could transform his curse into a true gift.

Thus, Lucas found himself alone, with his visions as his only company. The pain of the divorce added to the burden of his precognitive ability, bringing him to a breaking point. However, in his solitude, he also found a new determination. He knew he had to understand his gift, not only for his own peace of mind but also to prevent his suffering from continuing to affect those he loved.

This new purpose led him to embark on his journey to Toledo, seeking answers among his ancestors and the stories of his family. He needed to discover how his visions could be a force for good, how he could transform his curse into a true gift. In the heart of Spain, among the shadows of ancient Toledo, Lucas hoped to find the keys to unravel his destiny and finally find the peace he longed for.

Days before his departure, Lucas had a terrifying and macabre premonition of the final fate of his ex-wife's new lover. While packing his belongings, he saw a light-colored Porsche Carrera GT speeding recklessly. In the vision, Claribel's lover was visibly furious. How could he not be with such an unpredictable woman as her? At 95 miles per hour, the car weaved dangerously through traffic. Suddenly, the driver made a sharp right turn on a narrow curve, not noticing that the lane was blocked by a huge, stopped truck. The impact was like crashing into a concrete wall at full speed. The force of the collision turned the car's seatbelt into a blade that sliced through the lover's sternum and abdomen, causing an instant and brutal death.

The scene was gruesome: the lungs, heart, and abdominal viscera were scattered, eviscerated, and exposed. The victim's face showed a stroke of surprise, frozen in an expression of disbelief and horror at the sudden arrival of death. One of the paramedics, with a macabre sense of timing, took a photo of the horrific accident and shared it on social media, fueling the morbid curiosity of those who wished to see the tragedy.

This vision, which left Lucas shaken, materialized twenty-four hours later, just as he landed at Barajas Airport.

II

During the flight to Madrid, Lucas was still unaware of the catastrophic, though foreseeable, death of the macho who had been his ex-wife's lover. Sitting by the window, he watched the clouds as memories of his journey as a visionary in this endearing world swirled in his mind. He recalled at least a couple of unforgettable episodes, moments that defined his life and that now, in the silence of the flight, seemed to take on new relevance.

He remembered vividly and with sadness how, on one occasion, while dining at the Chotis de Avila, savoring a sumptuous turbot in asparagus sauce, Lucas had a vision. Both sitting with their glasses of Albariño, Lucas momentarily went into a trance and saw how two individuals entered the establishment with short weapons hidden in their attire. Their target was a prominent lawyer who was with his colleagues, drinking a cognac.

In the vision, the individuals entered with terrifying precision, firing two shots at the smallest, baldest lawyer in the group, known as Orlando. One shot struck his head, the other his heart. After the murder, the men aimed at the onlookers as they passed, exited the establishment, and got into a BMW M3, leaving a trail of carbon monoxide in their wake.

The vision greatly disturbed Lucas, who began to shake uncontrollably.

—"Lucas! What's wrong? You're shaking..." —Claribel exclaimed, her face full of concern.

—"Nothing, it's a vision..." —Lucas murmured softly, trying to calm himself.

—"Another one? This has to stop. You need to get help, Lucas".

With a trembling voice, Lucas told Claribel about the premonition, detailing every unsettling aspect of what he had seen. Claribel listened with wide eyes, a mix of skepticism and terror crossing her face.

Not even four minutes passed when, through a glass window beside their table, Lucas saw two individuals enter the restaurant. The scene unfolded exactly as in his vision: two gunshots echoed in the establishment, paralyzing everyone present. Screams filled the air as someone called for an ambulance for the lifeless body of Orlando, the lawyer.

Lucas's precognition had come true to the letter, filling Claribel with palpable terror. The scene was imbued with an aura of mystery and dread as Lucas's reality and visions intertwined in a disturbing manner.

—"This is... impossible!" —murmured Claribel, her eyes wide, looking at Lucas as if he had suddenly become a stranger.

Lucas, still trembling, knew that his visions could no longer be ignored. Terror and uncertainty had permanently settled in their lives, and the need to understand and control his gift became more urgent than ever.

In a second round of situations, while savoring a cup of coffee, Lucas experienced another disturbing astral foretelling. This time, he saw how a doctor, a personal friend of his, was taking judo classes with a burly, untrustworthy man. She, married with two teenage children, was known for her beauty and dedication to hypertrophying her muscles with weights.

In the vision, while practicing judo holds, the doctor received all sorts of inappropriate massages in her private areas. The judo class turned into a session of caresses, followed by kisses, gasps, and finally, an intimate union. All this while the doctor's husband, also a doctor, was unaware of what was happening. Someone, as always, was recording the scenes to fuel the morbid curiosity, sending the husband a video of the final act between the judo master and his wife.

In the vision, the jealous husband took a gun and shot the doctor in the head, followed by a personal shot to the temple.

Shocked and torn by his vision, Lucas knew he had to act. He decided to call his friend and warn her, leaving a message on her voicemail. Unfortunately, though she read the message, she did not have time to act. Her husband came home with the video in hand, and after a fierce confrontation where she admitted the impudent acts, the jealous husband shot his wife in the head, followed by a shot to himself. The scene ended with two bodies on the ground, surrounded by an eerie silence.

The police, bewildered by the accuracy of Lucas's prediction, interrogated him intensely. They bombarded him with questions about how he could have foreseen what had happened minutes before. However, the interrogation did not progress, as the officers quickly noticed that Lucas was a wretched man, trapped in a whirlwind of visions they labeled as transient madness. The mystery surrounding his premonitions remained unsolved, leaving everyone with a sense of poetic uncertainty and terror.

In those mental sunsets, our main character found himself when the Iberia plane landed at Barajas Airport. The disturbing visions and painful memories swirled in his mind like persistent shadows. It was ten-thirty in the morning, and the seven-and-a-half-hour flight had been a journey of introspection and anguish for Lucas.

As the plane descended, Lucas couldn't shake the feeling of unease that had accompanied him throughout the flight. The vibration of the wheels touching down momentarily snapped him out of his thoughts, but the fog of his premonitions still enveloped him. He disembarked the plane with a tired body and an exhausted mind, knowing that Madrid, with its bustle and frenetic life, would be a temporary refuge and a possible source of new visions.

Passengers quickly dispersed, but Lucas lingered for a few moments on the walkway, inhaling deeply and trying to regain his composure. He knew his visions would not stop and that each day would bring new images, some as terrible as those he had already witnessed. Terror and uncertainty were now his constant companions, and arriving in Madrid would not change that.

As he moved toward the exit, Lucas couldn't help but remember Claribel's last words before they parted. "You need to get help, Lucas." But he knew that his gift, or curse, was not something that could be easily explained to a therapist. The line between reality and premonitions blurred more and more, and with each new vision, the terror became more palpable.

He knew this because he had visited a psychotherapist to explain the condition he was suffering from. The professional had attended to him and given him the best advice about his problem, which was serious and premonitory in every way.

The memory of that visit was fresh in his mind. He had entered the office with a mix of hope and skepticism. The psychotherapist, a middle-aged man with a sympathetic look and a calming voice, received him kindly. Lucas explained his visions, how they appeared without warning and came true with chilling precision.

—"What you're describing is very unusual, Lucas," the psychotherapist said after listening attentively. "However, we need to approach this from multiple perspectives. First and foremost, it's crucial that you find a way to manage the stress and anxiety these visions cause you."

He recommended practicing relaxation and meditation techniques, suggesting that being consciously present and fully focused at the moment of acting could help reduce anxiety. He also spoke about the importance of keeping a journal where Lucas could note each vision, trying to identify patterns that might give him more control over his gift.

—"It's essential that you don't let these experiences dominate your life," the therapist continued.

—"While we can't deny that your visions have come true, we need to work on how you can live with them without letting them negatively affect your emotional well-being."

Lucas nodded, mentally noting each piece of advice. However, when he left the office, the reality of his visions soon eclipsed any attempt to put the therapist's recommendations into practice. The images were too vivid, the terror too real. The idea of sitting down to meditate when he could be witnessing a disastrous future seemed almost absurd.

As he moved toward the exit of Barajas Airport, a shiver ran down his spine at the therapist's words. He knew he needed to find a way to control his visions, or at least understand them, to face the future without the constant fear of what he might see next.

As he left the airport, with the feeling that something terrible was about to happen never leaving him, he realized he had underestimated the need to follow the therapist's advice. The visions of violent deaths and betrayals mixed with everyday reality, creating an atmosphere of constant tension and mystery. Madrid awaited him, but so did the next mental sunset, filled with terror and premonitions, and Lucas knew he had to find a way to face his fears if he wanted to regain control over his life.

Barajas, with its hustle and constant flow of travelers, seemed indifferent to Lucas's internal struggle. The bright lights and public address announcements created a surreal contrast with the dark world of his premonitions. He knew he needed to find a way to control his visions, or at least understand them, to face the future without the constant fear of what he might see next.

Using a Renfe train from Atocha Station, Lucas took a high-speed train, arriving in Toledo half an hour later. Once at the Toledo bus station, he took a bus to Consuegra, which was an hour-long journey.

During his journey from the city center of Toledo, known as the city of three cultures or the imperial city due to the coexistence of Christians, Muslims, and Jews for centuries, Lucas had one of the most unforgettable premonitions of his life.

It was about an explosion that was going to occur at Atocha station a few hours later. In the vision, Lucas found himself in the bustling Atocha train station in Madrid. It was early in the morning, and the dawn light was just beginning to illuminate the city. The station was full of hurried people, individuals of all ages going to their jobs, students carrying backpacks, and travelers from all over.

Suddenly, a sense of imminent danger enveloped him. He felt that something terrible was about to happen. He saw several backpacks being discreetly placed in different trains. The carriers of those backpacks seemed like ordinary people, but Lucas could sense the evil in their intentions. In the vision, the backpacks exploded with devastating force, filling the station with smoke, screams, and chaos. The bodies of passengers were thrown through the air, and blood stained the walls and floor. The sound of sirens and the cries of pain and terror mixed into an infernal cacophony.

The intensity of the vision made Lucas wake up abruptly, gasping and covered in cold sweat. The other passengers did not seem to notice his distress, absorbed in their own routines. Lucas looked out the window, trying to find solace in the passing landscape, but the image of the destroyed Atocha station remained etched in his mind.

As the bus moved towards Consuegra, the weight of the premonition became unbearable. He knew he had to do something about his vision. The urgency to prevent the disaster consumed him, but he also knew how difficult it would be to convince someone of the reality of his premonition. Terror and uncertainty had permanently settled in his life, and Lucas understood that he had to find a way to face his fears and act, despite the skepticism he might face.

If he had stood up screaming that something was going to happen at Atocha, he would have been met with indifference.

The one-hour journey ended, and Lucas got off the bus in Consuegra with a feeling of weight on his shoulders. The tranquility of the small town contrasted with the chaos he had seen in his vision, but Lucas knew he could not afford to ignore what he had witnessed. He had to find a way to make himself heard and to prevent the tragedy at Atocha station from becoming a reality.

Unfortunately, the attack on Atocha station happened hours after Lucas had seen it in his vision. The explosions occurred exactly as he had premonished: with terrifying precision, the backpacks full of explosives detonated, filling the air with smoke and screams. The bodies of the passengers were thrown through the air, and blood stained the walls and floor. Chaos and despair took over the station, while the sirens of ambulances and police echoed in the distance.

Lucas, devastated by not having been able to prevent the disaster, was trapped in a cycle of guilt and despair. He knew that his premonitions were an immense burden, and although he had tried to warn the authorities, skepticism and disbelief had prevented any action. Now, with the tragedy consummated, Lucas had to face the consequences of his gift, seeking a way to live with the certainty that he had seen the future and had been unable to change it.

III

The lineage of Lucas's ancestors, the Presagios, traced back to ancient times in the old village of Consuegra, in Toledo. Still alive, though nearly a centenarian, Lucas's grandmother, Flora Presagios, remained the undisputed matriarch of an extensive and ramified family.

—"I've been waiting for you, my son," said the old Flora, her voice a whispering melody fading into the air.

Sitting in a room filled with history, surrounded by noble walnut cabinets exuding a scent of chiforobi, old paintings from remote eras, and almost prehistoric utensils, Flora was a symbol of resilience. At her feet, wrapped in sheets to relieve the chronic lumbago of her advanced age, she rested with dignity.

Flora, with her ninety-eight springs, had hair as white as silver and skin as clear as sea foam. Her speech was slow, but her small, piercing eyes still had the power to see beyond the visible, as if her eyes were windows to the past. Because Flora had the gift, an ancient legacy that ran through the veins of the Presagios, allowing her to see and feel what others could not. This gift was both a blessing and a burden, deeply connecting her with the secrets and mysteries of her lineage.

On Calle del Arco de Consuegra stands Flora's manor house, a residence that seems trapped in time. The stone facade, firm and venerable, is adorned with vines climbing up to the wrought-iron balconies. The windows, framed with carved wood, have dark shutters contrasting with the light tone of the stone. The main door, robust and adorned with iron studs, leads to a hallway that takes you to the heart of the house. Above the entrance, a small niche houses the image of a saint, a silent guardian that has witnessed the passage of generations of the Presagios.

Crossing the threshold, a wide interior courtyard unfolds, a haven of peace with ceramic tile floors forming geometric mosaics. In the center, an ancient well is surrounded by pots of geraniums and jasmine, whose flowers fill the air with their fragrance. The rooms, spacious and bright, have high ceilings with exposed wooden beams and walls decorated with tapestries and portraits of ancestors. The kitchen, with its stone fireplace and copper utensils, is the beating heart of the house, where Flora prepares traditional recipes passed down through generations. This house is not just a structure; it is a living witness to family history, a place where every corner holds memories and secrets of the Presagios lineage.

In the main hall of Flora's house hangs the coat of arms of the Presagios lineage, a piece that radiates history and solemnity. Softly illuminated by a candle that burns perpetually, the coat of arms is a testament to family pride and heritage. Forged in iron and gold, the coat of arms features an intricate design: in the center, an owl with piercing eyes, a symbol of wisdom and vigilance, majestically perched on an olive branch, representing peace and longevity. Surrounding the owl, four quarters alternate between deep blue and bright gold, each adorned with ancient symbols narrating the family's feats and legends.

The candlelight, flickering with a warm and steady glow, casts dancing shadows on the coat of arms, bringing the details to life. The edge of the shield, decorated with an intricate pattern of laurel leaves and flowers, shimmers faintly, reflecting the light with a touch of mystery. Just below, a crimson velvet ribbon bears the Presagios motto, written in ancient Latin: "Sapientia et Veritas" (Wisdom and Truth). The presence of the coat of arms, illuminated by that inextinguishable flame, seems to watch over the room and everything that happens within it, as if the spirits of the ancestors are always present, guarding the secrets and legacy of their lineage.

Impressed by the historical beauty of the Presagios residence on Calle del Arco, Lucas could barely murmur upon arrival:

—"Blessing, Grandma."

—"God bless you, my son. Sit down, the journey has been long, and we have many things to discuss."

Lucas, still fascinated by the majesty of the room, sank into an old armchair facing the enigmatic family crest. He felt a mix of reverence and fear, aware that this symbol concealed unfathomable secrets and forces that had shaped his destiny.

The grandmother, a figure of authority whom time had transformed into a pillar of wisdom, watched him with a mix of tenderness and concern. It had been two decades since they had seen each other, and although the years had passed, the bond between them remained intact, as powerful as on the first day.

—"Lucas, my dear boy, I know what you're going through. You can't keep suffering like this. The visionary curse that torments you is not a senseless punishment. It has a purpose, a reason that we must unravel together."

Lucas's eyes turned towards the family crest, resting on the owl that dominated its center. That owl, an ancient symbol representing the letter "M" in Egyptian hieroglyphics, was the guardian of his misery. The creature's piercing eyes foreshadowed what would happen moments before it occurred, a gift

Lucas had inherited that condemned him to an existence of anguished premonitions.

With surprising agility for her age, Grandma Flora approached an old adjoining cabinet. From it, she extracted a book of a venerable appearance, its pages yellowed and worn with use. She opened it with reverential care and searched through its pages until she found what she was looking for.

—"This book, Lucas, has been passed down from generation to generation. Here are the keys to understanding and mastering our gift. It's time for you to learn how to control it, to use it to your advantage and not as a burden. Together, we will unravel the mysteries of our family and break the chains that bind you to that dark destiny."

Lucas felt a spark of hope ignite within him. For the first time, the prospect of facing his destiny did not seem like an insurmountable task. With his grandmother's guidance and the ancestral knowledge contained in that book, perhaps, just perhaps, he could find the peace he so desperately sought.

Grandma Flora began to read aloud, her voice trembling but firm, filling the room with ancient and powerful words. And so, on that afternoon filled with history and mysticism, Lucas embarked on a journey towards self-knowledge and liberation, determined to transform his curse into a source of strength and wisdom.

The venerable tome, stained with mold, contained letters and narratives from the entire Presagios family, dating back to Don Santiago, detailing incidents of the gift of foresight. From the 17th century to the present millennium, the handwritten letters recounted extraordinary incidents, paralleling the famous premonition of Abraham Lincoln in 1865 about his assassination.

A perfect book for a magician of the illusion of precognition. Each page of the book was steeped in time, with worn edges and moisture stains that spoke of its age. The earliest letters dated back to the late 17th century, with elegant and meticulous handwriting. Don Santiago, the ancestor who had started this compilation, narrated his first visions with a mix of awe and fear. In a letter dated 1689, he described how he had accurately predicted a devastating fire that swept through the town's market. His words, though carefully chosen, conveyed palpable anguish, a desire to understand and perhaps free himself from that gift.

In a letter dated October 1700, Don Santiago detailed the vision he had of the death of King Charles II of Spain. In his dream, he saw the monarch lying in his bed, surrounded by courtiers and doctors who were vainly trying to save his life. The spectral figure of Death, with its gleaming scythe, loomed over the king, marking the end of his reign. Don Santiago described how he had woken up with a start, certain that the vision was an imminent premonition. Barely a month later, on November 1, 1700, the news of King Charles II's death spread throughout Spain, confirming the terrible vision that had tormented Don Santiago. His letter, written with trembling handwriting, reflected both awe and resignation at the power of his gift, a power that allowed him to see the future but not change it.

As Grandma Flora continued reading, Lucas could almost feel the weight of centuries and the experiences of his ancestors. In later letters, the narratives became more detailed and occasionally desperate. A letter from 1745 recounted the vision of a tragic duel, while another from 1812 precisely described a storm that wreaked havoc in the region.

Among these family stories, some resonated with broader historical events. An entry from 1865 described the disturbing premonition of one of his ancestors about the assassination of Abraham Lincoln. The letter, written in agitated prose, detailed how the family member had seen the assassination in a vivid dream, days before it occurred. This connection to such a significant event made the family's gift feel both a blessing and an inescapable curse.

The more recent letters, from the 20th and 21st centuries, showed an evolution in the understanding and management of the gift. There were descriptions of dreams and visions related to natural disasters, wars, and significant personal events. A few pages were dedicated to philosophical and spiritual reflections on the nature of time and destiny, written with a maturity that reflected years of contemplation and suffering.

Grandma Flora gently closed the book, letting the echo of the past resonate in the room. Her eyes, full of wisdom and compassion, met Lucas's.

—"This book, Lucas, has been passed down from generation to generation. Here are the keys to understanding and mastering our gift. It's time for you to learn how to control it, to use it to your advantage and not as a burden. Together, we will unravel the mysteries of our family and break the chains that bind you to that dark destiny."

Lucas felt a spark of hope ignite within him. For the first time, the prospect of facing his destiny did not seem like an insurmountable task. With his grandmother's guidance and the ancestral knowledge contained in that book, perhaps, just perhaps, he could find the peace he so desperately sought.

And so, on that afternoon steeped in history and mysticism, Lucas began a journey towards self-knowledge and liberation, determined to transform his curse into a source of strength and wisdom.

Grandma Flora ordered some Spanish porridge and Manchego cheese to be prepared so the poor man could have dinner. The cook, a woman with skilled hands and a kind smile, quickly got to work, knowing well the importance of that meal. The aroma of roasted chickling pea flour with garlic and bacon soon filled the house, while the cheese, perfectly cured, awaited on a ceramic plate adorned with traditional motifs.

Accompanied by a good red wine from La Mancha, a succulent blend of Tempranillo, Garnacha, and Cabernet Sauvignon grapes, Lucas prepared to eat. The wine, deep and robust, reflected the arid land and sunny vineyards of the region. Its fruity and spicy notes intertwined perfectly with the rustic flavors of the Spanish porridge and cheese.

Grandma Flora, sitting across from him, watched his every move with the wisdom of someone who has lived much and understood more. She knew that only in sobriety did the gift manifest. As long as there was some alcohol in his blood, the visions were considerably subdued, giving Lucas a temporary respite from the premonitions that haunted him.

—"Lucas, my son," said Grandma Flora softly, "you can't hide from your destiny forever. The wine gives you a break, but it can't be a permanent solution. We must learn to control this gift, to live with it."

Lucas nodded as he took a sip of the dark wine, feeling the warmth of the alcohol spread through his body, easing the weight of the visions. Since childhood, he had learned that wine was a refuge, a shield against the flashes of inevitable futures that appeared without warning. But he also knew his grandmother was right. He couldn't run away forever.

Grandma Flora began to read again from the tome, her voice intertwining with the crackling of the fireplace and the gentle murmur of the Toledano night. Stories of past visions, of ancestors who had faced similar storms, filled the room. Each story, a lesson; each premonition, an echo of his own.

—"In this letter," said Grandma Flora, pointing to a yellowed page, "Don Santiago predicted the death of King Charles II in 1700. He too sought solace in wine, but found peace by accepting his gift, by facing it with courage."

Lucas listened intently, feeling how his grandmother's words and his ancestors' stories began to form a guide, a path to follow. The food and wine gave him strength, but it was the ancestral wisdom that provided hope.

That night, as the moon rose over the windmills of Consuegra, Lucas felt a little more prepared to face his destiny. With the support of his grandmother and his family's legacy, he began to envision a future where his gift would not be a curse but a powerful tool to understand and perhaps change the world around him.

IV

The morning light gently entered through the kitchen windows, creating a cozy and warm atmosphere. Grandma, an early riser by habit, had prepared a breakfast that celebrated the flavors and traditions of the region.

On the rustic wooden table, a feast awaited Lucas. There were slices of freshly baked bread, with a crispy crust and a fluffy interior. To one side, a plate of extra virgin olive oil, with a golden green hue, ready to be generously spread on the bread. Next to it, bowls of crushed tomatoes, seasoned with salt and garlic, emitted a fresh and irresistible aroma.

Also, on the table were slices of perfectly cured serrano ham and a plate of Manchego cheese, cut into thin wedges that showed its firm texture and ivory color. Some scrambled eggs, made with Grandma's traditional recipe, fluffy and golden, steamed invitingly on a ceramic plate.

There were also olives, picked from nearby olive groves and marinated with aromatic herbs, offering a perfect contrast of flavor. To accompany, there was a jug of freshly made coffee, its aroma filling the kitchen, and a selection of natural juices, orange, and peach, freshly squeezed.

In a corner of the table, a small basket contained fresh fruits: grapes, apples, and pears, adding a touch of natural sweetness to the breakfast.

Grandma, with a serene smile, served Lucas a cup of coffee and offered him a slice of bread with tomato and ham. The first bite was a feast of flavors, a celebration of the simplicity and quality of the ingredients.

After breakfast, Lucas decided to explore Consuegra. He departed from his grandmother's residence on Calle del Arco, ready to immerse himself in the history and charm of the city.

Walking through the cobblestone streets, he felt a deep connection with the place. The fresh morning air carried the scent of freshly baked bread and the echo of distant conversations. Lucas first headed to Spain Square, the heart of Consuegra. The wide, open square was surrounded by historic buildings with balconies adorned with flowers. In the center, the Fuente de los Leones rose majestically, a work of art representing the strength and history of the city.

He continued his walk toward the Castle of Consuegra, an imposing medieval fortress that stood atop a hill. As he approached, Lucas couldn't help but feel overwhelmed by the magnitude and age of the structure. The stone towers and walls, worn by time, told stories of battles and conquests. He climbed the winding path to the main entrance, where the panoramic views of the La Mancha plain took his breath away. From there, he could see the famous windmills stretching along the ridge of the hill.

Lucas decided to visit one of these windmills, which had inspired the adventures of Don Quixote in Cervantes's novels. The most famous one, known as Molino Rucio, was open to the public. Inside, he found a small museum explaining the workings of the mills and their importance to the region's economy. The enormous blades turned slowly, moved by the constant breeze that caressed the hills.

Descending the hill, Lucas headed to the Ermita del Santissimo Christ de la Vera Cruz, a small church dating from the 16th century. The hermitage, with its simple yet elegant architecture, was a place of peace and reflection. Inside, the walls were adorned with frescoes and ex-votos, witnesses of the faith and devotion of generations of Consuegra's inhabitants. Lucas lit a candle in honor of his ancestors, feeling a deep spiritual connection.

From there, his steps took him to the Municipal Archaeological Museum, where artifacts telling the story of Consuegra from pre-Roman times to the Middle Ages were displayed. The objects on display, from ancient tools to pieces of pottery and coins, offered a fascinating insight into the city's evolution. Lucas stopped in front of a showcase containing a collection of medieval weapons, imagining his ancestors defending the city in times of war.

Finally, Lucas decided to conclude his tour at the Tercia Palace, a historic building that had served as a grain storehouse and later as a noble residence. The palace's architecture, with its sturdy walls and elegant details, reflected the wealth and power of its inhabitants. As he walked through its rooms, Lucas could almost hear the whispers of voices from the past, intertwining with the echoes of his own premonitions.

He returned to his grandmother's residence as the evening fell, with his mind full of images and the feeling of having traveled through time. Each monument, each corner of Consuegra, had left a mark on his soul, reminding him that his family's history was intrinsically linked to that of the city. Lucas knew that, like the ancient walls of the castle, he too had to find the strength to endure and thrive.

Once more, after exploring the town of Consuegra, Lucas returned to his grandmother's house. The day had been long and full of revelations, but he knew there was still much more to discover in the ancient tome of the Presagios family. He sat at the old oak table, where the book lay open, its yellowed pages full of secrets waiting to be unraveled. The ancient book of the Presagios, along with the entire family history, awaited him.

Grandma, always perceptive, brought him a cup of herbal tea and sat beside him. Together, they began to delve into episodes of the family's predictive history, exploring how some of these premonitions had been resolved by knowing in advance what was going to happen.

Lucas ran his fingers over a particularly worn page and began to read aloud. It was an entry from the year 1723, written by an ancestor named Manuel de los Presagios. Manuel had had a disturbing vision of a collapse in a local mine, threatening the lives of many workers. Thanks to the premonition, Manuel was able to warn the miners and prevent a catastrophe. The entry detailed Manuel's anguish in deciding how to act on his vision, the initial disbelief of the miners, and the relief he felt when the community was ultimately saved.

Each story read from the book was a lesson, each premonition an echo of his own. The tales of how his ancestors had faced and sometimes altered the outcomes of their visions filled Lucas with a sense of purpose. He realized that his gift, though burdensome, also held the potential for great good.

Continuing with his exploration, Lucas found another entry from 1804. This time, the prediction had been made by his great-great-grandmother Isabela. She had seen a devastating fire that would ravage much of Consuegra. Using her vision, Isabela managed to convince the mayor of the need to create a fire prevention system and additional water stores. When the fire actually began, the preventive measures saved countless lives and properties. Isabela became a respected and revered figure in the community for her bravery and foresight.

Each page of the tome revealed stories of premonitions that had altered the course of events. In 1856, a distant uncle named Felipe had foreseen a severe drought that would threaten the region's crops. Thanks to his warning, the farmers were able to store enough water and ration their resources, mitigating the effects of the drought and ensuring the community's survival.

Lucas found particularly fascinating an entry from 1932, where his grandfather Ernesto had a vision of a train accident. Ernesto worked tirelessly to understand the details of his premonition, eventually deciphering the location and time of the disaster. With this information, he was able to alert the railway authorities, who took preventive measures to avoid the accident, thus saving hundreds of lives.

As Lucas read these stories, he couldn't help but feel inspired and burdened with responsibility. Each account was a testament to the power and burden of his gift, and how his ancestors had struggled with the same duality of premonition and action. He felt that the book was not just a record of visions but a manual on how to use his gift for good.

Grandma, observing his absorption in the reading, said softly, "Lucas, our family has been both blessed and cursed with this gift. Each generation has found its way to face and use it. You are no different. With knowledge and wisdom, you can turn these visions into something positive, something that can save and guide."

Lucas nodded, deeply moved by his grandmother's words and the stories he had just read. He closed the tome reverently, knowing that his journey was just beginning. He felt a renewed determination to understand and master his gift, using the lessons of the past to forge his own path.

That night, as the wind whispered through the old trees outside the house, Lucas fell asleep with a sense of purpose. He knew he had a mission, and with his grandmother's support and his family's ancestral knowledge, he was prepared to face any challenge the future held.

V

After his morning walk, Lucas entered his grandmother's house, inhaling the familiar aroma of herbs and spices that always greeted him. In the corner of the living room, his grandmother, a woman with small eyes and gentle hands, awaited him with a warm smile.

—"Come, Lucas, sit beside me" —she said, indicating the old velvet armchair by the fire.

Lucas obeyed, feeling a mix of curiosity and anxiety.

—"Grandma, how did you control your premonitions?" —he asked, his voice barely a whisper.

She smiled and took an ancient leather-bound book from a nearby shelf.

—"This book has been passed down through generations in our family. It contains the secrets and techniques our ancestors used to manage the gift".

Lucas took the book carefully, feeling the weight of history in his hands. Grandma opened a page marked with a red ribbon and began to read aloud:

—"To control the gift, you must first learn to calm your mind. Meditation is the key. Close your eyes and listen only to your breath".

As his grandmother guided Lucas through a meditation session, he felt an unfamiliar calm take over him. The images and sounds of his premonitions became clearer, less overwhelming. When he finally opened his eyes, his grandmother handed him a small silver amulet.

—"This will help you focus your visions —she said, placing the amulet in his hand—. Carry it with you always".

Lucas observed the silver amulet in the palm of his hand, admiring the intricate details on its surface.

—"This amulet belonged to Don Santiago, your great-great-grandfather" —his grandmother explained, her voice filled with reverence—.

—"He forged this amulet, imbued it with the knowledge and energy necessary to help you control your visions".

Holding the amulet, Lucas felt a warm vibration course through his body. He closed his eyes and took a deep breath, letting the amulet's energy envelop him. Gradually, the blurry and chaotic images of his premonitions began to focus, revealing clear details that had previously eluded him.

—"When you feel overwhelmed, hold the amulet, and concentrate on its energy" — said his grandmother, gently placing it around Lucas's neck—.

—"It will help you channel your visions and protect you from negative influences".

Lucas marveled at the craftsmanship of the silver amulet. The afternoon light reflected off its surface, highlighting the intricate patterns that adorned its front. The engravings formed a hypnotic mandala, with interwoven lines creating a design that seemed to move and change with each turn of the amulet.

—"This amulet has been in our family for generations" —said his grandmother, observing the fascination in Lucas's eyes—.

—"The symbols around the edge represent the elements of nature. They were engraved by your great-great-grandfather, Don Santiago, to protect and guide those in our family who possess the gift".

In the center of the amulet, a white quartz stone captured the light, projecting tiny rainbows around it. Lucas ran his fingers over the amethyst crystals surrounding the quartz, feeling a gentle vibration that resonated with his own energy.

—"The back has even more significance" — continued his grandmother, turning the amulet to show him the tree of life engraved on the silver—.

—"This tree symbolizes our roots and connection to our ancestors. The inscription in Latin, '*Per scientiam et sapientiam, praemoneo,*' reminds you that it is through knowledge and wisdom that you will control your visions".

Lucas felt the solid weight of the amulet in his hand, a comforting sensation that gave him newfound confidence. He put it around his neck, feeling the coolness of the silver against his skin. He closed his eyes and took a deep breath, allowing the amulet's energy to merge with his own. With his grandmother's guidance and the ancestral power of the amulet, he knew he was ready to face his premonitions with a new sense of control and purpose.

Lucas nodded, feeling a new hope bloom in his chest. With his grandmother's guidance and the power of ancestral knowledge, he knew he could learn to control his gift. With Don Santiago's amulet hanging over his chest, he knew he had the tool necessary to master his gift. Sitting by the fire, with his grandmother by his side, Lucas closed his eyes and plunged into a deep meditation, the amulet glowing softly with a silvery light.

With Don Santiago's amulet hanging over his chest, Lucas felt more prepared than ever to face his premonitions. However, he knew he needed more tools to control his gift. So, in addition to his grandmother's lessons, he decided to incorporate new practices into his daily routine.

Lucas walked down Calle del Arco; his mind filled with the recent teachings of his grandmother. As he reached the end of the street, he turned towards Parque del Molino Viejo, a place that had always provided him with peace and clarity.

The park was in its prime, with lush green grass and cherry trees beginning to bloom. As he entered, the restored old mill caught his eye, a majestic structure standing like a guardian of the past. Lucas always found comfort in the history that the mill represented, a tangible connection to his ancestors and their traditions.

He found his favorite bench, located near one of the small ponds where ducks swam peacefully. He sat down, closed his eyes, and began his visualization practice. The gentle sound of the fountain water and the light breeze rustling the leaves of the trees helped him focus.

Holding Don Santiago's silver amulet in his hand, Lucas felt a wave of calming energy flow through his body. He entered a state of deep meditation, visualizing his premonitions with renewed clarity. Every detail, every image, became sharper and more controlled under the soothing influence of the environment.

Parque del Molino Viejo had become his personal sanctuary, a place where he could disconnect from the outside world and focus on mastering his gift. With each visit, he felt closer to understanding and controlling his premonitions, thanks to the combination of his grandmother's teachings, the power of the amulet, and the serenity of the park.

He closed his eyes, concentrating on his breathing. With each inhalation, he let go of stress and anxiety, allowing his mind to clear. As he exhaled, he visualized his premonitions with renewed clarity, gently guiding them as if they were scenes from a movie.

One after another, dark forces tried to carve their way into Lucas's psyche. He felt their presence as cold shadows, clawing at the edges of his mind. However, thanks to his grandmother's guidance and Don Santiago's silver amulet, a unique cosmic force surrounded him, protecting him.

This force was not visible, but its presence was unmistakable. When Lucas closed his eyes and concentrated, he could feel this luminous energy flowing through him, forming an impenetrable shield. The shadows struck against this barrier, unable to breach it. The tranquility this protection afforded him allowed him to focus his thoughts and visions, keeping him safe from the malevolent influences that sought to invade his mind.

Lucas knew that this cosmic force was the result of his family's ancient magic, combined with his own will and determination. With each passing day, he felt his control over this energy grow, giving him the confidence needed to face any challenge his premonitions might bring.

In the afternoons, he attended Tai Chi classes at the community center. The smooth, controlled movements, along with rhythmic breathing, gave him a new sense of balance and control over his body and mind.

Each class was an opportunity to strengthen his connection between body and spirit.

Lucas also became an avid reader of ancient texts and mythology. He spent hours in the library, fascinated by stories of ancient seers and their methods for controlling their gifts. He noted down any interesting techniques in his notebook, eager to try new strategies.

At night, he wrote in his journal, reflecting on his day's experiences. He described his visions in detail, along with his emotions and thoughts. This process of self-reflection helped him identify patterns and better understand how his emotional states influenced his premonitions.

Finally, he found an online group of people with psychic abilities. He participated in discussions and attended virtual workshops, where he learned from the experiences of others and shared his own progress and challenges.

With each new practice, Lucas felt he gained a little more control over his gift. Although he knew the journey would not be easy, he was determined to master his premonitions.

VI

Practice makes perfection. This maxim, repeated throughout the centuries, has proven its validity countless times. However, verifying its absolute truth can be an unpredictable challenge. What was evident to Lucas, though, was that as he perfected his control over his premonitions, he began to master the emotions associated with each of them.

Each vision brought with it a torrent of feelings: fear, anxiety, hope. At first, these emotions overwhelmed him, clouding his ability to understand and act upon his premonitions. But over time, and thanks to his grandmother's teachings and the protection of Don Santiago's amulet, Lucas learned to channel these emotions and use them to his advantage.

He visualized a cosmic ring around each spiritual idea attempting to manifest in his mind. This ring not only surrounded them but also filtered their entry, acting as a tollgate that decided which premonitions could cross and which remained outside. It was a control mechanism that granted him immense power over his own gift.

When a premonition tried to break into his mind, the cosmic ring evaluated its importance and relevance. The most urgent and significant visions managed to pass through, while trivial or disturbing ones remained outside, unable to penetrate his mental barrier. This system not only gave him control over his visions but also allowed him to maintain inner peace, consciously deciding which spiritual influences he allowed into his cosmic mind.

Thanks to this control, Lucas could focus his energies on the premonitions that truly mattered, those that could change the course of events. With each passing day, his mastery over this cosmic ring strengthened, making him feel more secure and powerful in his ability to foresee and manage the future.

Lucas came to understand that his gift was that of a true time traveler. Einstein's theory of relativity, that colossal effort to unravel the mysteries of the universe, manifested in his ability to predict the future with astonishing precision. Lucas was not just a mere seer; he was a transient time traveler, a privileged observer of what was to come.

Each time a premonition enveloped him, Lucas found himself transported into a vivid, pulsating movie. He moved within that movie, detail by detail, becoming part of its fabric, interacting with the characters, and feeling the texture of the future with visceral intensity. It was a fascinating and terrifying spectacle at the same time, where he was both actor and spectator, until, for some reason he still did not fully understand, he was abruptly pulled from the scene. The movie continued without him, following its inexorable course toward the unknown that only he knew.

Imagine for a moment the reach of such a gift for the future of humanity. The potential to foresee events, to understand and perhaps alter destiny, was unimaginable. In the wrong hands, that gift could have been a tool of immense power and devastation. The military, always hungry for strategic advantage, would have kidnapped him without a second thought in times of war. They would have used him to feed their artificial intelligence systems, to predict enemy movements, and uncover their weaknesses with terrifying accuracy.

Lucas, however, understood the weight of his responsibility. He was not merely an instrument of prediction; he was a guardian of possible futures. As he faced the enormity of his gift, he sought ways to use it for good, conscious that each premonition, each journey through time, was not just a vision but an opportunity to influence the destiny of humanity.

He was ready. He felt deep within his being that he needed to return to his homeland, to that corner of the world where it all began. His grandmother, the pillar of his childhood; his past, a canvas of intertwined memories; the book of premonitions, a source of ancestral wisdom; and his grandfather's amulet, protector of his restless spirit, had restored the peace he had longed for. It was time to shed the shadows of yesterday and move forward into an uncertain but promising future.

However, destiny, with its inscrutable designs, always has the final word. It spreads its capricious kindness and alters the story of our lives, taking us to remote and uninhabitable places, forging paths we never would have imagined. As Lucas stood in the park, a sad premonition invaded his mind and heart, tearing him from his momentary serenity. He saw his grandmother bidding farewell to this world, having completed her mission of guiding the last of the lineage bearing the gift of foresight.

That night, in a dream scented with the intoxicating aroma of red roses, the spirit of his grandmother ascended to the right hand of our Lord. It was four in the morning, the hour when the possibilities of dreaming multiply, when the pressure of the eye is greatest, the eye of life. Lucas woke up at that precise moment, feeling his grandmother's departure like a whisper in his soul, a gentle breeze that announced her farewell.

Only angels move at that hour of the morning.

There she was, beautiful in her final rest, wrapped in mortuary sheets like a shrouded queen. Her eyes, though closed forever, reflected a deep serenity, while her spirit remained alive, aware of each goodbye. Lucas was the first to approach, his heart shattered into a thousand pieces, his eyes flooded with tears. He looked at his grandmother's face and, with unshakable certainty, knew that her spirit was more present than ever.

—"Thank you, Grandma," he whispered, his voice trembling.

With a final kiss, sweet and salty from tears, he bid farewell, watching as she entered the tunnel of light from which many never wish to return. He saw her leave, taking a part of him with her, but also leaving behind a legacy of love and wisdom that would guide his steps forever.

Unexpectedly, his grandmother had left the historic residence on Calle de los Arco's in Consuegra to Lucas in her will. It was a medieval castle, a fortress built of stone and mystery. Now, Lucas was not only the owner of those imposing walls but also of the enigmatic Book of Premonitions, an ancestral tome whose power and secrets had been guarded for generations. He was the last of the lineage unless he sired descendants.

There he was, our protagonist, immersed in the gloom of the great hall, contemplating his future with the intensity of someone facing a vital crossroads. The decision was not simple: to stay in the ancestral abode that offered a tangible link to his roots or return to his homeland, where his life, though less grand, was simpler and more familiar. That was the question, a dilemma that seemed to split his soul into two irreconcilable halves.

Lucas slowly walked through the corridors, gently touching the walls that held the echoes of bygone times. The torches crackled in their iron candelabras, casting dancing shadows that seemed to whisper in his ear. With each step, he felt the weight of history on his shoulders, the burden of a legacy calling him to stay and uncover the secrets the castle hid.

From the high tower, he could see the town of Consuegra stretching beyond the walls. Its inhabitants, unaware of Lucas's inner conflicts, continued with their lives, small dots on a vast canvas he had to decide whether to leave or make his new home. The wind blew strongly from the north, bringing with it the scent of damp earth and the promise of coming storms, as if destiny itself spoke to him in an ancient and profound language.

In his mind, images of his childhood in distant lands mingled with visions of the future in the castle. He remembered his mother's laughter, his father's warm embrace, and the certainty of a place he could always call home. Now, facing the majesty of his grandmother's legacy, he understood that time does not stand still and that every decision has the power to change the course of his life forever.

The night advanced, and with it, Lucas's decision seemed more imminent. He sat on the stone throne that dominated the main hall, the Book of Premonitions resting heavily in his hands. He knew that whatever his choice, he must face it with courage and determination, honoring the memory of his ancestors and forging his own path in the vast tapestry of history.

For now, he had to attend to his grandmother's funeral services, which temporarily postponed his return. His grandmother had left explicit instructions: she wanted to be cremated and have her ashes rest in the family crypt at the Consuegra cemetery. This cemetery, located near the iconic Consuegra windmills on Cerro Calderico and the church of Santa María la Mayor, was a place rich in history and tradition.

The crypt, a sacred place for the family, already housed the cremated remains of Lucas's beloved grandfather. This site not only held the vestiges of his ancestors but also the memories of past loves, stories whispered through generations. Every stone, every corner, seemed to tell a chapter of the family history, and now, it would be the final resting place of his grandmother, thus sealing a cycle of life and death.

As Lucas organized the preparations, he felt the weight of heritage and the bond with his roots. His grandmother's decision to be cremated and eternally united with her husband in that place was an act of love that transcended death. In the silence of the cemetery, between the whisper of the wind caressing the mills and the solemn tolling of Santa María la Mayor's bells, Lucas found a strange comfort. It was as if, in that space between past and present, an eternal connection was woven, a reminder that life, though fleeting, always finds a way to perpetuate itself in the memory of those who remain.

The ceremony would be simple but full of meaning, a final farewell on the same ground that had witnessed so many family stories. As he placed the ashes in the crypt, Lucas would feel a mix of sadness and relief, knowing that his grandmother would finally be at peace, beside her beloved, in the place they both called home.

The farewell ceremony for Lucas's grandmother was held with solemnity and emotion. Family and friends gathered in the old Consuegra cemetery, where the gray sky and the mills on Cerro Calderico seemed to maintain a respectful silence. Under the shelter of Santa María la Mayor, the atmosphere filled with soft murmurs and melancholic glances. Lucas, with a heavy heart, spoke a few words of farewell, thanking his grandmother for the teachings and unconditional love she had always given him. The ashes, contained in a finely carved marble urn, were placed in the family crypt next to his grandfather's remains, sealing a love that endured beyond life.

Despite deciding to return to his homeland, Lucas chose to take the Book of Premonitions with him, that mysterious legacy his grandmother had guarded so zealously. He felt that, although he was leaving behind the medieval castle and life in Consuegra, the book represented an unbreakable connection to his roots and family history. At the end of the ceremony, as the sun set behind the mills, Lucas embraced each of the attendees, promising never to forget his roots. With the book firmly in his hands, he understood that, although he was physically leaving, the premonitions and secrets of his lineage would remain a vital part of his existence, guiding his steps in the new chapter about to begin.

VII

From the narrow airplane window, Lucas watched the clouds passing below him, each one a silent witness to his wandering thoughts. He pondered what he would do once he returned to his homeland, where destiny, that invisible master orchestrating our lives, would rekindle his deepest memories. The hippocampus, that part of the brain responsible for memories and navigation, now seemed like a chest filled with uncertainties and hopes.

With the money Flora, his grandmother, had left him, Lucas could rent an apartment on the coast, where the waves of the Atlantic drew an imaginary line to Consuegra, uniting two worlds separated by the sea and time. That line, invisible but palpable, spoke to him of continuity and cycles that never end.

On the north coast, he found a two-bedroom house furnished with rustic and simple charm. The apartment, owned by a couple who had decided to spend some time in San Sebastián, offered a privileged view of the sea. From there, Lucas could gaze at the horizon, letting the ebb and flow of the waves whisper stories of ancient sailors and inspire him to write his own destiny. As he unpacked his belongings, including the enigmatic Book of Premonitions, he felt that, although he was starting a new chapter, he carried the weight and wisdom of his ancestors, prepared to face any omen the future might hold.

The time traveler opened his mental vault to the matters that emanated energy in the environment. He let it be seen that he was ready to navigate the intrinsic labyrinths of the spiritual space, where the arguments for things to come slip in. He became a sensor for future events, a kind of magnet for the electromagnetic waves that carry all kinds of thoughts. His mind, now tuned and receptive, absorbed every vibration, every whisper of the universe, interpreting the signals that presaged the coming events. Reality unfolded before him in overlapping layers of possibilities, and he, with an almost superhuman serenity, explored them all, aware that every choice, every movement, could alter the course of history itself.

Around that time, coinciding with Lucas's arrival in the coastal town, a tragic event shook the nearby community: a fair-skinned, blonde boy of only eight years old was found gravely injured in his home. His mother, desperate, took him to the hospital, where he was sadly declared dead. The authorities, upon starting the investigation, encountered inconsistencies in the statements of those present and forensic evidence that failed to provide a clear narrative of the events.

Lucas, with his unique premonition ability and guided by the visions from the Book of Premonitions, delved into the web of mystery surrounding the case. In one of his meditations, he had a disturbing vision: the boy had caught his older sister and her boyfriend under the sheets in an intimate moment. Alarmed, the boy had told them he would tell their mother everything.

—"¡I am going to tell Mom!"

It was then that the boyfriend, in a fit of panic and fury, grabbed a golf club that was in the room and hit the little boy on the head. The rest is history.

When he arrived at the headquarters to tell what he had seen, Lucas faced a wave of skepticism from the authorities. His accounts of premonitions and visions were met with disbelief and disdain.

—"Are we supposed to believe in visions and premonitions?" —said the chief detective, crossing his arms skeptically.

—"I know it sounds improbable —Lucas responded calmly—, but there's a detail that cannot be ignored". The golf club used in the attack has a specific mark, a dent that can only be seen by someone very close.

The detective frowned, exchanging looks with his colleagues.

—"A dent? —murmured one of the officers, clearly intrigued—. How can you be so sure?"

—"I saw it in my vision —Lucas affirmed firmly—. It's a detail that hasn't been mentioned anywhere. Check it, and you'll see I'm right".

Finally, the boy's sister, overwhelmed by the pressure and weight of the truth, confessed:

—"It was him, my boyfriend. My brother caught us, and he... he got scared" —she said through sobs, covering her face.

—"He hit him with the golf club so he wouldn't say anything".

The confession allowed the authorities to arrest the young man, the son of a prominent politician in the country, and thus solve a case that seemed destined to remain unsolved if the sister had not confessed to the crime. Thanks to Lucas's premonitory abilities, justice could prevail, bringing some peace to a community devastated by tragedy.

The resolution of this case became Lucas's calling card to the authorities. There had been so many people at the residence that day that it was difficult to determine who the murderer was. It was believed that a one-armed drifter who roamed the community had entered and, with the hand he didn't have, had struck the eight-year-old boy on the head. However, Lucas's intervention and premonitions unraveled the truth, revealing that the real culprit was much closer than anyone could have imagined.

It had been over twenty years since the disappearance of a three-year-old boy from a neighborhood in Caimito. The community had been shaken by the tragedy, and despite tireless searches and media attention, the case had gone cold, leaving the family with persistent pain and waning hope.

Lucas had felt a special connection to this case since he was a child. His abilities were not widely understood or accepted, but those few who knew him were aware that his visions were extraordinarily accurate.

One day, while meditating in his tranquil home, Lucas had a clear and detailed vision of what had truly happened that fateful afternoon. He saw the boy playing in the yard and then an unknown man sneaking up. The kidnapping had been an act of revenge; the man, filled with spite, took the boy to inflict pain on the family. In his vision, Lucas followed the kidnapper through the streets and into a car. Then, everything became blurry, and he was transported to a small town in the United States, where he saw the boy, now grown, living with a loving couple who, though they treated him as their own, had been complicit in the lie from the beginning.

Lucas knew he had to act quickly. With a racing heart, he went to the family of the missing boy and told them what he had seen. At first, there was skepticism, but desperation and hope intertwined, leading them to follow the clues Lucas had provided. They contacted local authorities and shared Lucas's vision, who described the town, the house, and the details he had seen with precision.

The authorities, intrigued by the accuracy of the description, decided to investigate. They traveled to the indicated place and, after some inquiries, found the young man. The couple who had raised him confessed through tears that they had done so out of love but under circumstances they knew were not right. The original kidnapper, a distant relative of theirs, had acted out of spite, and they had accepted to raise the child without asking questions.

The reunion between the young man and his biological family was emotional and complex. There was joy, pain, and many questions, but also a deep sense of relief. Lucas, observing from a distance, knew he had fulfilled his mission. He was neither a detective nor a policeman, but his visions had managed to solve a mystery that had tormented a community for decades. And though he knew the scars of the past would always remain, he also knew that the power of truth and reunification was a powerful force for healing.

A seven-year-old girl had disappeared from her neighborhood in a southern town, leaving the community shaken by the tragedy. Despite tireless search efforts and media attention, fifteen years passed, the case went cold, and the family was left trapped in persistent pain and agonizing hope.

One night, while meditating in his coastal apartment, Lucas had a powerful and heartbreaking vision. He saw the girl playing in front of her house on that fateful summer afternoon. Suddenly, a white van pulled up, and a man quickly got out, grabbing the girl and taking her with him. The vision grew darker and more confusing, but Lucas could follow the man to a house in an isolated neighborhood.

Determined to follow this lead, Lucas contacted the authorities and shared his vision. Although his methods were unconventional, the precision and desperation in his account were enough for the authorities to act. An operation was organized to investigate the house Lucas had described in such detail.

Upon arriving at the house, the owner, a man who had lived there for decades, denied any knowledge of the girl's disappearance. However, using dogs, the police began digging in the backyard, following Lucas's exact description. Soon they found skeletal remains buried shallowly. DNA tests confirmed what the girl's family had feared for so long: the remains belonged to the missing girl.

The news shook the community and brought a mixture of pain and relief to the family. Although finding the remains meant the girl would not return, they could at least start to close that painful chapter of their lives. The homeowner was arrested and, under interrogation, confessed to the crime. He had kept that dark secret for years, living with the guilt of his atrocious act.

Lucas, observing from a distance, knew he had fulfilled his mission. His visions had managed to solve a mystery that had tormented a community for decades. Although he knew the scars of the past would always remain, he also knew that the power of truth and justice was a powerful force for healing.

The girl's case was finally resolved, thanks to Lucas's intervention and his extraordinary abilities. The community, though marked by tragedy, found a new sense of unity and strength, always remembering the girl and the importance of protecting the most vulnerable.

Little by little, Lucas delved into the shadowy, labyrinthine realms of unresolved cases, those that had remained suspended in a limbo of uncertainty and pain. He did so with a clear mission: to provide metaphysical and spiritual help, shedding light on the darkest corners where the truth had been hidden.

Lucas possessed an extraordinary gift, a gift that set him apart from ordinary mortals. He was capable of seeing the invisible, of perceiving what had been forgotten or ignored by time and memory. Beyond simple perception, he had the ability to control these visions, focusing them with the precision of a watchmaker adjusting the most delicate gears of an antique clock. Thanks to this, he could unravel secrets that would never have been revealed, weaving together scattered fragments of the past to reconstruct broken stories.

VIII

The apartment that Lucas rented offered an impressive 180-degree panoramic view of the vast Atlantic Ocean from a height of 56 feet. The sea, in its splendor, displayed a range of blue and turquoise hues, shades owed to the presence of phytoplankton, those tiny unicellular marine algae that, in high concentrations, tinted the ocean with their characteristic green color. This corner of the world, with its serenity and natural beauty, was a refuge of peace for Lucas. However, despite the tranquility the place provided, human needs and hormones continued to dictate their own terms, and Lucas felt a growing urge to find a companion.

Loneliness was beginning to weigh on him, and although he longed for companionship, he knew it couldn't be someone with the unusual characteristics of Claribel. After the tragic accident in which her boyfriend lost his life in a Porsche, Claribel had been left emotionally devastated, and their relationship had become a constant reminder of pain and loss.

Lucas clearly remembered the tumultuous days that followed the accident. Claribel, with her exuberant energy and imposing presence, had been a dazzling figure in his life. However, the tragedy had transformed her. Her vivacity had faded, replaced by a deep sadness that time seemed incapable of healing. Lucas realized he needed someone different, someone who could bring light into his life without the weight of such a painful past.

As he watched the ebb and flow of the waves, Lucas reflected on the type of person he desired by his side. He wanted someone who could share his appreciation for the beauty and tranquility of the sea, someone with whom he could have deep and meaningful conversations, and with whom he could build a connection based on mutual understanding and compassion.

The ocean view stretched out to the horizon, a constant reminder that the world was full of possibilities. Lucas decided he wouldn't rush his search. In his heart, he knew that finding the right person would take time, but he was also convinced that somewhere, someone was waiting for him, someone who could fill the void in his life and share the peace he had found in his seaside home.

Thus, Lucas prepared to open his heart once more, ready to welcome a new companion, someone who, like the ocean, would bring with them a tide of new hopes and shared dreams.

A few apartments below where Lucas lived, there was a woman named Laura Valeriano. Known professionally as Dr. Valeriano, Laura specialized in psychoanalysis and paranormal phenomena, including premonitions. Destiny had placed her in Lucas's path, with the intention that they both could better understand the dual aspects of the gift of precognition, the yin and yang of this extraordinary ability.

Laura was a slender and petite woman, endowed with a charming smile and clear eyes that radiated deep understanding. Like Lucas, she lived facing the beach in the same apartment complex. She had chosen her apartment with exquisite taste, decorating it in a way that enhanced the turquoise of her eyes and the misty white of her perfectly aligned teeth.

One afternoon, while they were both on Lucas's terrace, watching the ocean, Laura broke the silence.

—"Have you ever thought about what it would be like to live without the premonitions?" —asked Laura, her clear eyes reflecting the light of the sunset. Lucas sighed and looked at the horizon.

—"Sometimes. But I also realize that, without them, I wouldn't be who I am today. And you? What is it like helping people like me?", Laura smiled softly.

—"It's challenging, but also incredibly rewarding. Seeing someone find peace and understanding amidst the chaos of their visions is a gift in itself".

Their initial encounters with Lucas were fortuitous but revealing. As they got to know each other, they realized they shared a special connection. Laura, with her experience in dealing with paranormal phenomena, offered Lucas a new and comforting perspective on his visions. Her presence, always serene and understanding, provided Lucas with a sense of peace and stability he had never known before.

—"Sometimes I feel like my visions are consuming me" —confessed Lucas during one of their sessions.

—"I don't know how to deal with them".

—"You're not alone in this, Lucas" — responded Laura with firmness.

—"We'll find a way to manage it together. It's a matter of balance and accepting that this gift can be both a burden and a blessing".

Laura not only understood the challenges that Lucas faced, but she also guided him with wisdom and patience. Together, they explored the depths of his gift, seeking to balance the premonitions with everyday life. Laura taught Lucas to see his abilities as a gift rather than a curse, showing him how to find the balance between knowledge of the future and acceptance of the present.

—"Remember, Lucas —said Laura one day, as they walked along the beach. —Every vision is an opportunity to learn something new about yourself and the world. Don't fear what you see; use it to grow and to help others".

Every day, as the sun set over the ocean, the two would meet on Lucas's terrace, sharing stories and visions, and strengthening the bond that united them. The relationship between Lucas and Laura flourished, nourished by mutual understanding and the desire to help each other navigate the turbulent waters of precognition. Together, they embarked on a journey of self-discovery and support, learning to manage their gifts while building a life full of promise and possibility.

After several months of an intimate relationship, Laura became pregnant with Lucas. The news filled them with a mix of joy and anticipation; both were eager to have their first child. With hearts pounding and emotions running high, they decided to share the news with Lucas's mother, the daughter of the venerable Flora. Doña Jimena, a woman of firm convictions and deep-rooted traditions, received the news with a mix of pride and concern.

—"¡You both have to get married! that baby cannot be born a bastard". —had stipulated Doña Jimena, her voice resonating with the authority of generations.

The imperative tone of Doña Jimena left no room for doubt. For her, marriage was a matter of family honor and respect. Lucas and Laura understood the importance of her words and decided to follow her advice. Thus, with the determination of those who know their actions transcend personal bounds to become part of their lineage's history, they planned the ceremony.

A month later, Lucas's beachfront apartment was transformed into the setting for an intimate yet symbolic wedding. Under a clear sky and with the murmur of the ocean as a witness, a few close guests gathered, and a legal cleric officiated the ceremony. The atmosphere was imbued with a solemn serenity, as if each wave breaking on the shore accompanied the vows that were about to be spoken.

The apartment, decorated with wildflowers and soft lights, filled with a cozy warmth. The few attendees, carefully selected for their closeness and significance in the lives of the couple, settled in the main room, creating an intimate and familial environment. Lucas, dressed in an elegant light suit, and Laura, radiant in a simple but beautiful white dress, looked at each other with a mix of love and determination.

The cleric, a man of wise words and deep gaze, began the ceremony with a brief reflection on love and commitment. His words resonated in the room, blending with the sound of the waves and the gentle whisper of the wind. Lucas and Laura held hands, feeling the energy and emotion of the moment.

—"Today, in the presence of these witnesses and under the benevolent gaze of nature, Lucas and Laura join in marriage" —said the cleric, his voice firm and serene.

The vows were spoken with a sincerity that moved everyone present. Lucas promised to love and care for Laura, respecting and valuing each day together. Laura, with tears of happiness in her eyes, made her promises, reflecting the depth of her feelings and her unwavering commitment.

—"Now, by the power vested in me, I declare you husband and wife —announced the cleric, sealing the bond with a blessing".

A soft, emotion-filled applause broke the silence, and the newlyweds melted into a kiss that symbolized the beginning of a new chapter in their lives. The ceremony, though simple, was a perfect reflection of their love and commitment, uniting not just two people but also their histories and hopes.

That night, under a starry sky and with the rhythmic sound of the sea as their background music, Lucas and Laura celebrated their union. The sea breeze caressed their faces as they danced barefoot on the sand, feeling the deep connection between themselves and the world around them. The presence of their loved ones and the blessing of their natural surroundings made that moment eternal, forever etched in their hearts and in the history of their shared lives.

Officially, Laura moved to live with her husband, Lucas, in his apartment by the sea. She carried within her the promise of new life, a child that would take another eight months to be born. With each passing day, anticipation and joy mixed with the serenity of the place as they awaited the arrival of their firstborn.

Thus, on the twenty-third of December, a day that seemed chosen by destiny itself, their son was born. It was seven in the evening on a Sunday when the cry of a six-pound baby boy broke the silence. The light of the sunset softly filtered through the windows, illuminating the moment with a golden warmth.

The baby was blond, with clear eyes reflecting the innocence and purity of his arrival into the world. His hair, surprisingly, appeared already styled, a detail that brought smiles and tears of joy to those present. From the first moment, his voice resonated with strength, demanding the nourishment that Laura, with her full breast and heart overflowing with love, quickly provided.

Laura, reclining in bed, looked at her son with a mixture of awe and tenderness. Lucas, by her side, could not contain his overwhelming emotion. The small family united in an unbreakable bond of love, feeling that this moment marked the beginning of a new chapter in their lives.

The apartment, which had witnessed so many nights of reflection and moments of intimacy, filled with a new energy. Every corner seemed to vibrate with the presence of the newborn, and every detail took on new significance. The ocean waves, once a constant murmur, now seemed to sing a lullaby, soothing the baby in his first days of life.

During the first weeks, Laura and Lucas devoted themselves entirely to their son. Every cry, every laugh, every gaze from the little one was a discovery, a new page in the book of their family life. Laura, with her maternal instinct, became the pillar of the small family, while Lucas, with his unwavering support and love, strengthened the bonds that united them.

Their daily routine transformed into a harmonious dance of care and attention. The nights filled with frequent awakenings, with whispers and soft songs to calm the baby. The days slipped by with warm baths, walks on the beach, and moments of shared tranquility. Each gesture, each caress, each word of love built a haven of security and affection for the newborn.

Thus, life in the apartment by the sea was enriched by the presence of the child, who with his clear eyes and blond hair, brought new light to Lucas and Laura's days. United by love and shared responsibility, they began to weave the threads of a family story that intertwined with the constant murmur of the ocean, a silent witness to their happiness and hope.

At four months old, the baby began to emit incomprehensible melodies, small whistles, and hums that seemed to arise from a deep and mysterious place. These notes, although lacking clear meaning for the adults, captivated the attention of all who heard and saw the child. There was something in his gaze, in the way his clear eyes lit up as he produced these sounds, that suggested a connection to something beyond the tangible.

There was no doubt that this firstborn had the gift of the Presagios. The melodies that came from his lips were not mere infant babblings but early manifestations of an ancestral ability that ran through his veins. Lucas and Laura watched with a mix of awe and reverence, aware of the burden and blessing this signified.

The apartment, already transformed by the baby's arrival, now vibrated with a new energy. The child's incomprehensible melodies mingled with the ocean's murmur, creating a unique symphony that filled every corner of the home. The days passed with a constant sense of wonder as the parents strove to understand and support the development of this special gift.

One afternoon, as Laura cradled the baby in her arms, she noticed how his tiny fingers seemed to follow an invisible rhythm, a subtle dance accompanying his hums. Lucas, watching from the doorway, felt a surge of pride and responsibility. He knew that, as a father, he had the duty to guide his son in understanding and mastering his gift, just as his own ancestors had done.

—"It's incredible, Lucas —murmured Laura, her eyes full of tenderness and concern".

—"Our son has the gift, I see it in every one of his gestures, in every one of his melodies".

Lucas nodded, stepping closer to place a hand on Laura's shoulder.

—"I know, and we will do everything possible to help him grow up understanding and valuing this gift. He will not be alone in this".

As time went by, the baby's melodies became an integral part of daily life. The neighbors, intrigued by the strange sounds that often floated up to their windows, began to wonder about the origin of those enchanting notes. Visits became more frequent, each person eager to witness the miracle firsthand.

Laura and Lucas, aware of the curiosity and attention their son's gift was generating, decided to be discreet. They understood that this gift was both a blessing and a responsibility, and they wanted to ensure their son grew up in an environment of love and understanding, away from exploitation or misunderstanding.

Thus, every night, as the baby's melodies filled the air and the stars shone over the ocean, Lucas and Laura renewed their commitment to protect and guide their son. The gift of Prophecy, a powerful and mysterious inheritance, had found a new manifestation in their firstborn, bringing new hope and new challenges for the family.

In the warm refuge of their seaside home, the three of them huddled together, knowing that the road ahead would be full of discoveries, learning, and undoubtedly, the incomprehensible melodies that would continue to enchant and challenge all who heard them.

Grandmother Jimena, Lucas's mother, came almost every day to take care of the baby. She spent hours rocking him, singing softly, and observing his every movement with unconditional love. Jimena knew her days were numbered as an undiagnosed malignancy spread through her old body, slowly eating away at her vitality. However, in every moment shared with her grandson, she found deep solace, a reason to keep going.

When Lucas and Laura's son was two years old, Jimena said goodbye to this world. A definitive diagnosis of multiple myeloma, followed by a visit to a renowned oncology clinic that gave up on her, was enough to mark the beginning of the end. On Tuesday, November 17, surrounded by the love of her family, Jimena was buried, leaving an impossible-to-fill void in the hearts of Lucas and his family.

Lucas was left motherless, and his son without a beloved grandmother. This event, laden with pain and loss, could not have been foreseen by Lucas, despite his gift. The inability to have anticipated and thus helped his mother during the short three-month ordeal after the fateful diagnosis caused him immense suffering.

—"Dearest mom, how I wish I could have done something, seen this coming" —Lucas murmured as tears fell down his face, remembering Jimena's last days.

Laura, always by his side, offered comfort, though she also shared the pain of the loss.

—"You did everything you could, Lucas. Your mother knew how much you loved her".

Jimena's daily visits to the seaside apartment became a sacred ritual. Her hands, though already weakened, rocking him, were a symbol of love and dedication. Her voice, soft and maternal, was a constant source of tranquility for the baby. Every laugh and every little gesture of the child were a balm for Jimena, who saw in him the continuity of life, a promise of future amidst her personal battle against the illness.

The diagnosis of multiple myeloma came as a devastating blow. The family, stunned and overwhelmed by the news, threw themselves into seeking all possible treatment options. But visits to the oncology clinic and medical consultations only confirmed the inevitable. Jimena, with stoic serenity, accepted her fate, dedicating her last months to enjoying her family's company and planting indelible memories in them.

In her final days, Lucas and Laura took turns staying by Jimena's side, listening to her stories, learning from her wisdom, and cherishing every moment. The house filled with a palpable melancholy, while the sound of the waves continued their relentless ebb and flow, indifferent to human pain. The little one, not fully understanding what was happening, continued to offer smiles and melodies, unaware of the gravity of the situation.

On the day of the funeral, a cold breeze swept across the beach. The ceremony was simple but deeply emotional. Lucas, standing beside his mother's grave, felt the weight of the loss, a mix of sadness and resignation. As the earth covered the coffin, a part of him seemed to be buried as well, a part that only Jimena could understand and heal.

Despite his gift, Lucas found himself trapped in helplessness. Not having been able to foresee his mother's illness, not having been able to intervene and prolong her life, left a deep wound. His ability to anticipate the future had not been enough to save the one he loved most, and that thought tormented him day and night.

In the days that followed, the house by the sea felt strangely empty. Jimena's absence was a void that neither the child's laughter nor the ocean's songs could fill. However, amidst that pain, Lucas and Laura found a new determination. They decided to honor Jimena's memory by caring for their son with the same love and dedication she had shown.

Jimena's loss marked a before and after in the family's life. Strengthened by his mother's example, Lucas vowed to protect and guide his son on the path of the gift of Prophecy, ensuring he grew up in an environment full of love and understanding. Although the pain of the loss would always be present, so would Jimena's legacy, a source of inspiration and strength for future generations.

IX

Now, at four years old, Julián Presagios showed signs of being a prodigy in premonitions. Lucas had seen it in the small visions his son shared, visions of surprising clarity and precision for someone so young. However, there was a shadow darkening this bright future: a black hole indicating an adverse event in the family's life, something Lucas couldn't decipher with certainty.

Lucas was in his study, reviewing some old family documents, when he felt the familiar twinge in his head that preceded a vision. He closed his eyes and, as so many times before, let himself be carried away by the stream of images that flooded his mind.

The scene unfolded quickly before him. He saw his son Julián, just four years old, playing in the backyard of their house. It was a sunny afternoon, and the sounds of birds singing and the gentle wind caressing the leaves of the trees filled the air. Julián laughed as he chased a butterfly, his laughter innocent and carefree.

Suddenly, the atmosphere changed. A dark van appeared, and several hooded men dressed in black emerged from it. They moved quickly and silently, like shadows. Lucas felt a wave of terror as he saw one of the men approach Julián and grab him roughly. The child started to scream, his laughter transforming into cries of fear.

Lucas tried to move, tried to shout, but he was trapped in the vision, helpless. He watched as the men shoved Julián into the van and quickly disappeared. Despair and panic filled Lucas's heart as the vision faded, leaving him back in his study, gasping and covered in cold sweat.

He opened his eyes and found himself back in reality, but the feeling of terror remained. He knew that what he had seen was a premonition of the future, a future he had to prevent at all costs. His son was in danger, and he had to act quickly to save him.

Lucas jumped up and ran to Julián's room. When he opened the door, his heart sank. The bed was empty, the sheets rumpled, and the window wide open. Julián's favorite teddy bear lay on the floor, crushed.

A chill ran down his spine as the reality set in his vision had not been a warning of what was to come, but a representation of what had already happened. Julián had been kidnapped.

Desperate, Lucas ran to the garden. He saw recent tire marks on the grass and small footprints disappearing in the direction of the driveway. His mind raced, trying to remember every detail of the vision to find any clue that could help locate his son.

He pulled out his phone with trembling hands and called the police. —My son has been kidnapped! —he shouted, trying to stay calm enough to give the necessary details—. Julián Presagios, four years old, has just been taken in a dark van. I think I know where they're taking him.

After hanging up, he dialed the number of his best friend, Antonio, a former police officer with experience in crisis situations.

—"Antonio, I need your help" —said Lucas, his voice breaking when his friend answered—. "Julián has been kidnapped. I have a vision of where they might be taking him".

Antonio needed no further explanation. He knew Lucas's gift well and knew that his visions always came true. —I'm on my way, Lucas. Don't worry, we'll find Julián.

As he waited for Antonio, Lucas tried to calm down and focus. He closed his eyes and held his great-grandfather's amulet, trying to catch any trace of his son's presence. He had to remember every detail of the vision: the tattoo on the kidnapper's arm, the partial license plate of the van, and any other clues that could help track down the culprits.

When Antonio arrived, they both quickly headed to the place Lucas had seen in his vision. They knew every second counted and that they had to act with speed and precision. As they drove, Lucas told Antonio everything he had seen and felt, trying to reconstruct the scenario in his mind.

—"We'll find him, Lucas" —said Antonio with determination—. "We won't let them get away with this".

Lucas nodded, grateful for his friend's presence and the implicit promise of support. With his heart filled with hope and fear, he prepared to face any danger to save his son. He knew that his gift was both a blessing and a curse, but at that moment, the only thing that mattered was Julián.

Suddenly, he heard the sound of a car approaching rapidly down the driveway. Laura, his wife, was returning from the clinic she ran. Lucas felt a knot in his stomach at the thought of breaking the news to her.

Laura parked the car and hurried into the house, noticing the agitation in the atmosphere.

—"What's going on, Lucas?" —she asked, concern in her voice as she saw her husband's expression.

Lucas swallowed hard, trying to find the right words.

—"Laura... Julián has been kidnapped" —he finally said, his voice breaking with pain.

Laura froze, unable to process what she had just heard. —What? —she murmured, her voice barely a whisper. Then, understanding the magnitude of Lucas's words, she began to cry inconsolably, her sobs filling the room.

—"Why? —she cried out between tears—. Why would anyone want to kidnap a four-year-old child?"

Lucas embraced her, trying to comfort her while he himself struggled to hold back his own tears.

—"I don't know, Laura. But we will find him. We won't let them get away with this".

Laura nodded weakly, trusting in Lucas's determination. She knew her husband would do everything possible to save their son. As Antonio arrived and the authorities began to mobilize, Lucas and Laura prepared to face the greatest challenge of their lives, united in their love and desperation to get Julián back.

Lucas was trying to calm Laura when his phone rang, vibrating on the kitchen table. The sound resonated through the house, laden with tension. Lucas looked at the screen and saw that the call was from a blocked number. With a knot in his stomach, he answered.

—"Who is this?" —he asked, trying to keep his voice steady.

—"We have your son". —said a thick, ominous voice on the other end of the line. Lucas felt a chill run down his spine. The voice continued—. "Listen carefully, Lucas. This is what's going to happen".

Lucas gripped the phone tightly, his heart pounding violently. Laura, seeing her husband's expression, moved closer, her eyes filled with panic.

—"We're going to pull off a spectacular heist at the city museum tonight" —the voice continued, cold and calculating—. "We kidnapped your son to ensure you don't have any visions about the robbery. Julián is our guarantee that you won't interfere. If you have a vision and share it with anyone, you'll never see your son again".

Lucas's world crumbled further. He knew he couldn't let the kidnappers carry out their plan, but his son's well-being was at stake. — What do you want from me? —he asked, trying to buy time and gather more information.

—"We just want you to stay out of our business —the voice responded"—. Don't get involved. If you do, Julián will pay the price. We'll make sure you never see him again.

—"Don't hurt him!" —Lucas begged; his voice filled with desperation—. "Please, I'll do whatever you want, but don't hurt my son".

The voice laughed, a sinister sound that made Lucas's skin crawl.

—"That depends on you, Lucas. Keep your mouth shut and everything will be fine. We'll call with further instructions. And remember, not a word to the police".

The call ended abruptly, leaving Lucas with a racing heart and trembling hands. He slowly lowered the phone, trying to process what had just happened.

Laura looked at him with tear-filled eyes.

—"What are we going to do, Lucas? We can't let them get away with this, but we can't risk Julián's life either".

Lucas clenched his teeth, his mind racing to find a solution.

—"We need to find a way to save Julián and stop those men without them knowing we're acting".

Antonio arrived at that moment, hurrying through the door.

—"What's going on, Lucas? What did they say?"

Lucas quickly explained the situation, his voice filled with anguish and determination. Antonio nodded, understanding the gravity of the matter.

—"We're going to need help" —said Antonio.

—"I know some trusted people who can help us track these guys without alerting them. If we can find out where they're holding Julián, we can act before they realize what's happening".

Lucas nodded, feeling a spark of hope.

—"Yes, we need to do this quickly. We can't let these monsters get away with it".

As Antonio contacted his former colleagues, Lucas closed his eyes again, clutching his great-grandfather's amulet. He tried to focus, searching for any trace of a new vision that could help them find Julián. He knew that every second counted, and he wouldn't rest until his son was safely back home.

Laura, by his side, tried to stay strong, her love and fear for Julián giving her strength. She knew their family was in danger, but she also knew that together they could overcome anything.

That night, as Lucas, Laura, and Antonio worked frantically to track down Julián's whereabouts, the kidnappers' plan went into motion. Several robbers, dressed in black and moving with coordinated precision, stormed the city museum. With military-like accuracy, they neutralized the security guards and disabled the alarms, heading straight for their preselected targets.

In a matter of minutes, they took two famous paintings valued at four million dollars. The masterpieces, national treasures, vanished without a trace. Additionally, the thieves stole historic jewels from the city's royal collection, invaluable pieces representing centuries of history and culture.

Lucas had foreseen this robbery, but he hadn't been able to reveal it to the authorities due to the threat to his son's life. The premonition had shown him every detail of the heist: the precise movements of the robbers, the objects that would be stolen, and the resulting chaos. However, Julián's kidnapping had forced him to stay silent, unable to act without risking his son's life.

As news of the robbery spread quickly through the city, Lucas felt trapped between despair and guilt. He knew he could have prevented the disaster, but Julián's well-being was his absolute priority.

Laura clung to Lucas, seeking comfort amidst the storm of emotions.

—"How are we going to find him, Lucas?" —she asked, her voice broken with anguish.

Antonio, who had been working tirelessly, returned with new information.

—"I've contacted some of my old colleagues. They traced the call from the blocked number and have a lead on where they might be holding Julián. We need to move fast".

—"Let's go —Lucas said, his voice steely with determination. —We're getting our son back".

Lucas nodded, feeling a spark of hope amidst the darkness. —Let's go, we can't waste any time.

They headed to the indicated location, an abandoned warehouse on the outskirts of the city. As they approached, Lucas felt a mix of fear and determination. He knew the kidnappers were dangerous, but he would not let them take his son away from him.

Antonio stopped at a safe distance from the warehouse and began planning their entry.

—"We need to be careful. We don't know how many there are or how they're armed. Lucas, have you had any visions about this place?"

Lucas closed his eyes and concentrated, holding his great-grandfather's amulet. Images began to form in his mind: he saw the interior of the warehouse, shadows moving, and heard Julián's voice calling him. His son was there, but there was also danger. He saw the warehouse empty; the kidnappers had left.

—"I've seen the inside —said Lucas, opening his eyes—. It looks like they've abandoned it, but Julián is inside. We need to hurry".

Antonio nodded, adjusting his jacket.

—"All right, follow my lead. We'll move quickly and silently".

With hearts pounding, they approached the warehouse. Antonio moved with the skill of a professional, guiding Lucas and Laura with precise signals. They reached the entrance and found the door ajar. Antonio pushed it open slowly, revealing the dark and empty interior of the warehouse.

They entered the warehouse and found Julián in a back room, tied up but unharmed. The child's eyes lit up when he saw his parents, and tears of relief streamed down his cheeks. Laura ran to him, untying and hugging him tightly.

—"Mommy, Daddy... I was so scared" — Julián sobbed, clinging to them.

Lucas embraced him, feeling a tremendous weight lift from his shoulders.

—"We're here, son. You're safe now".

Antonio kept watch at the door, ensuring there were no kidnappers nearby. —It looks like they've gone. We need to get out of here before they come back —he said quietly.

With Julián in his arms, they headed towards the exit, moving carefully and quickly. As they left the warehouse behind, Lucas felt a deep gratitude for having recovered his son. He knew the battle wasn't over, but for now, they had achieved the impossible.

Once safe, Laura called the authorities, informing them of the warehouse location and the kidnapping. The police arrived quickly, finding the place empty but confirming it had been used recently. Although the kidnappers were gone, the information provided by Lucas and Laura was crucial for the investigation.

Lucas, Laura, and Julián returned home, exhausted but relieved. They knew they still had much to process and that the consequences of the robbery would be significant, but for now, they were together and safe.

The authorities began tracking the clues left by the kidnappers. Footprints and other evidence in the warehouse allowed the police to identify some of the gang members. Arrest warrants were issued, and operations to capture them began.

With the help of the clues and additional visions from Lucas, the police managed to locate several of the kidnappers. In a series of coordinated raids, they arrested those responsible for the robbery and the kidnapping. During interrogations, it was revealed that the gang had connections to an international network of art and antiquities trafficking. The captured members provided valuable information about the leaders and operations of the network.

The authorities recovered the stolen paintings and historical jewels, returning them to the city museum. The news of the recovery was a relief to the community, though the trauma of Julián's kidnapping and the robbery left a deep mark on Lucas and his family.

Lucas, Laura, and Julián tried to return to normalcy, knowing they had gone through a terrifying experience but had come out stronger and more united. Lucas continued to use his gift to help the authorities in the fight against crime, determined to protect his family and other innocents from future dangers.

X

It had been a little over five years since Julian's kidnapping. Now, having become a ten-year-old pre-adolescent, Julián carried with him not only the memories of that traumatic event but also the growing awareness of his ability for premonitions. Like all members of the Presagios family, his gift was powerful but disorderly, sometimes confusing, and uncontrollable.

Lucas had observed with a mix of pride and concern how his son began to manifest his capacity for premonition. Julián's visions were sporadic and often disconcerting, but Lucas was determined to guide him and help him control his gift. He knew the best way to do this was by connecting him with his roots, with the history of his family. That's why he had decided to take Julián to Consuegra, the place where his grandmother Flora had lived, and which now belonged to them. Laura, Julián's mother, would also join the trip, seeking to support her family and connect with the Presagios legacy.

One sunny morning, Lucas, Laura, and Julián boarded the plane, ready for the trip. In

Madrid, they would take a train to Toledo and then a bus to Consuegra. Consuegra was not only a beautiful place, with its famous windmills and medieval castle, but it was also steeped in the history and heritage of the Presagios family.

—"Dad, what was Grandma Flora like?" — asked Julián as the plane soared through the air.

Lucas smiled, recalling his grandmother fondly.

—"She was a strong and wise woman. She had a very powerful gift, like you, and always said that our abilities were both a blessing and a responsibility. She spent a lot of time in Consuegra, studying and perfecting her gift. I'm sure you'll learn a lot there".

Laura, who had been listening attentively, added:

—"My grandmother Flora was an incredible person. I was fortunate to know her and learn from her. I'm sure this trip will help us understand our roots and your gift better, Julián".

The trip passed with family stories and laughter, with Julián asking questions about his heritage and his parents sharing memories and anecdotes. They arrived in Consuegra at sunset, with the sun tinting the sky a shade of orange and the windmills casting long shadows over the landscape.

Lucas parked the car in front of his grandmother's old house, a stone mansion with a history dating back centuries. As they got out of the car, Julián looked around, feeling a special connection to the place. Laura took her son's hand, smiling as she observed Julián's reaction.

—"This place is amazing, Dad —said Julián, his eyes shining with excitement—. I feel something... I don't know how to explain it, but it's like this place has something special".

Lucas nodded, understanding exactly what his son meant.

—"It's our family's history, Julián. This place is full of memories and energy. Let's go in and discover more".

As they entered the house, they were greeted by a mix of ancient aromas and the warmth of a home filled with history. The walls were adorned with family portraits and old tapestriés, and in the center of the main room, a large stone fireplace added a cozy touch to the atmosphere.

Lucas showed Laura and Julián the rooms and special corners of the house, sharing stories of his grandmother Flora and how she had used her gift to help others. Julián listened attentively, fascinated by the stories, and feeling increasingly connected to his heritage.

That night, they sat together in the living room in front of the Presagios family crest, enjoying a simple but delicious dinner. Laura looked at her family, feeling grateful for the opportunity to be together and explore their legacy.

—"It's important that we understand and embrace our history, Julián —said Laura softly—. This trip is not only to learn about your gift but also to strengthen us as a family".

Julián nodded, feeling the love and support of his parents. He knew he was not alone in his journey to understand and control his gift, and that gave him the strength to face any challenge that might arise.

That night, as they prepared for bed, Lucas took Julián to the room that had been his grandmother Flora's. The room was filled with old books, amulets, and objects that Flora had collected throughout her life.

—"This was your grandmother's favorite place —said Lucas—. This is where she studied and perfected her gift. I'm sure you will find much inspiration and knowledge here".

Julián looked around in awe, feeling his grandmother's presence in every corner.

—"Thank you, Dad. I promise I will do my best to learn and honor our heritage".

Lucas smiled and hugged his son.

—"I know, Julián. I'm very proud of you".

As Julián settled into bed, Lucas and Laura retired to their room, feeling more connected and strengthened as a family. They knew this trip was just the beginning of a new chapter in their lives, a chapter filled with discovery and growth.

That same night, Lucas brought Julián the amulet that his grandmother had given him before she died. Now it was his turn to carry it, bearing the weight of the great-grandfather until he had descendants, if he ever did. The full moon lit his path, creating long and mysterious shadows.

Entering the house, Lucas found Julián lying in his grandmother's bed. The room was full of memories, with old photographs and the persistent aroma of chiforobi. Lucas approached slowly, trying not to disturb the peace that still seemed to envelop the room.

—"Julián —Lucas whispered—, I have something for you".

Julián slowly opened his eyes and sat up, looking at the amulet that Lucas held in his hand.

—"Is that... the Amulet of the Descendants?"
—he asked, with a mix of wonder and nostalgia.

—"Yes —replied Lucas, sitting on the edge of the bed—. Now it's your turn to carry it".

Julián took the amulet carefully, feeling its weight in the palm of his hand.

—"I always thought it was just a legend —he said softly—, but now that it's here... it feels so real".

—"It's more than real —said Lucas—, it's a responsibility we carry in the family. It's not just an amulet; it's a legacy".

The two remained silent for a moment, sharing the weight of the past and the uncertainty of the future. The moon shone through the window, illuminating their faces and the amulet that now symbolized so much for both of them.

Although they had the ability to glimpse each other's future, they refrained from doing so. They did not wish to tarnish the fleeting joy found in the delicate moment of transition between two travelers of the perpetual and incessant river of time, that phenomenon that never stops, always moving forward and devouring everything in its path.

In that liminal space, between the past that no longer existed and the future that had yet to manifest, there was a fragile stillness, a pause in which the present dissolved into a symphony of unrealized possibilities. It was there, in that interlude, where time travelers found a kind of solace, a momentary respite from the inevitable march forward.

The travelers crossed paths, sometimes exchanging a furtive glance, aware of the weight of knowledge each carried. It was a tacit pact, a shared acceptance that the charm of their journey lay in the uncertainty, in not knowing, in letting destiny reveal itself without interference. To break that veil was to betray the very essence of their nomadic existence through the ages.

Thus, they walked in parallel, immersed in their own thoughts and memories, letting time envelop and transport them, respecting the mystery and beauty of each transient moment. In the silence of those shared moments, there was a profound understanding, an implicit union, for both knew that time, though immortal and always moving, was also fragile and had to be approached with the reverence it deserved.

The clocks marked their relentless rhythm, but in those intertwined moments, time seemed to stand still, creating a space where the eternal and the ephemeral coexisted in a perpetual dance. And so, without looking into each other's future, they preserved the purity of their journey, allowing each step to be a revelation, each encounter a celebration of the infinite mystery that is time.

The Book of the Presagios was open to its last page. That page where Lucas began to write, and Julián began to live. The gift, though intermittent in some generations, persisted in the family, a heritage of power and mystery transmitted through time.

Lucas leaned over the book, his pen cutting through the silence of the night as he traced the words with almost ritual precision. Each presage he inscribed not only recounted his own story but also wove a tapestry for the descendants, a guide to understanding the special legacy that ran through their veins.

Lucas's words were not mere auguries but fragments of a deeper truth. They described the ability of some humans to possess special gifts, connected with the spirits of the earth, an affinity with invisible forces that shaped the destiny of the world. This spiritual connection was an invisible thread that united the members of his family through the centuries, a responsibility that each bearer had to accept and understand.

Julián, though still young, felt the weight of that responsibility. As Lucas wrote, he immersed himself in the reality of those presages, living them, feeling them as his own. Every word written by Lucas was an echo in Julián's mind, a reflection of his own future unfolding before him with unsettling clarity. He knew he could not escape this destiny, but he also understood that in his acceptance lay his true power.

The gift, with its capricious nature, had skipped generations, appearing, and disappearing like the tide. Some ancestors had experienced its influence only in fleeting glimpses, while others, like Lucas and now Julián, lived it intensely. The Book of the Presagios was the chronicle of this dance between the known and the unknown, a guide for those destined to follow this path.

Lucas looked up from the page, observing Julián with a mix of pride and concern.

—"This book —he said quietly— is more than a record. It is our connection to something greater than ourselves. You must understand and respect its power".

Julián nodded, feeling the weight of the book and his legacy.

—"I will —he replied, his voice firm. —I understand what this means".

It was the dawn of a new beginning.

As the night advanced, the two immersed themselves in the ritual of writing and understanding. Time seemed to stand still in that room, suspended between Lucas's words and Julián's life. Each line written was a promise, an eternal bond between past, present, and future, ensuring that the gift was never lost and that its power would continue to illuminate the path of those to come.

Lucas had felt the weight of his gift for as long as he could remember, a burden and a privilege that had accompanied him since birth. His first words, according to his parents, were not simple babbles but complete sentences that predicted future events. The gift of writing was not just a skill but a necessity, an uncontrollable urge that drew him to the Book of the Presagios, as if the blank pages were crying out for his ink.

Each night, while the world slept, Lucas found himself in the silent company of the book. The presages he wrote not only narrated the history of his family but also his own. The words flowed from his pen as if dictated by an invisible force, an intimate connection with the mysteries of time and destiny. In every stroke, in every line, Lucas saw his own life reflected, a life marked by the intersection between the human and the supernatural.

The clandestine truth lay hidden in the shadows of his writings: the author of these presages was not a mere chronicler, but a prophet trapped in the eternal cycle of writing. Lucas, from birth, had been the scribe of destiny, recording in the Book of the Presagios not only visions of the future but also the narrative of his own life, a life inevitably intertwined with the words he poured onto the paper.

In the silence of the night, black ink glided over the ancient paper, each word an echo of the inevitable fate. Lucas, pen in hand, was not just a writer but a medium between the known and the unknown, between reality and prophecy. The confines of his room dissolved into a sea of possibilities; each line drawn a step closer to the abyss of the inevitable.

The walls closed in around him, and the whisper of paper beneath his pen was the only constant in a perpetually changing world. Each prediction, each glimpse of the future, was a consuming truth, a reminder that his existence was inexorably entwined with the destiny of those he wrote about. And in that moment, the most hidden truth revealed itself only to him: Lucas did not merely predict the future; he lived it and recorded it, an eternal prisoner of his gift, both narrator and protagonist of a never-ending story.

* * *

About the Author

Born on April 14, 1954, in San Juan, Puerto Rico, Dr. Humberto Lugo Vicente, better known as Tito Lugo, is a distinguished figure in the field of pediatric surgery. His career has been marked by a fervent commitment to both medicine and the community he serves.

During his time at Colegio San José in Río Piedras, Dr. Lugo Vicente not only excelled in his studies but also led the local rock band "The Red Stones." He demonstrated exceptional skills in various areas, including music and martial arts, achieving black belts in Shotokan and brown belts in Taekwondo. His determination to fund his karate education by selling newspapers and taking on other jobs reflects his early commitment to his goals.

Graduating Magna Cum Laude in Sciences, specializing in Chemistry and Biochemistry, from the University of Puerto Rico, Dr. Lugo Vicente was honored with the Chemistry Medal and the Facundo Bueso Medal for his outstanding academic performance. He continued to excel in his medical studies at the same university, graduating as a member of Alpha Omega Alpha, the medical honor society.

Dr. Lugo Vicente has made significant contributions to pediatric surgery throughout his career. He completed his specialization in General and Pediatric Surgery at the University of Puerto Rico and then joined the faculty as a Professor of Pediatric Surgery. His dedication to excellence in education led him to hold various leadership positions, including President of the Medical Faculty and Director of the Surgery Department at the University Pediatric Hospital.

Dr. Lugo Vicente has been a tireless advocate for improving medical services in Puerto Rico, particularly in his efforts to equip the University Pediatric Hospital with modern operating rooms. This has benefited countless children and families.

Outside of his medical career, he enjoys a fulfilling family life with his wife, Wanda Torres Otero, and their four children: Karlos, Alex, Javier, and María del Carmen. His dedication to community well-being and his passion for medicine continue to inspire new generations.

Currently, Dr. Lugo Vicente practices at his private office in San Jorge Hospital and the University Pediatric Hospital. There, he provides quality medical care while cultivating his interests in oil painting, writing, and oenology, always maintaining the balance and moderation that characterize his life philosophy.

Other Novels by the Author
https://www.amazon.com/author/titolugo.md

1- Aquamistic (Spanish and English)
2- El Gran Sueño / The Great Dream
3- Marca de Faraón / Mark of Pharaoh
4- La Isla del Retiro / The Island of Retirement
5- Espejismos en la Red / Digital Deceptions
6- Voces del Silencio / Voices of Silence
7- Travos... (Spanish and English)
8- Misericordia Letal / Lethal Mercy
9- Pirulo... (Spanish and English)
10- ...Elipsis... / ...Ellipsis...
11- Precognición / Precognition